CHARACTERS

The following are a list of the main characters in this book, the majority of whom you met in Oregon Bound - book 1.

Thomspon family:
Pa - Paddy Thompson
Ma - Della Thompson
Eva - now Mrs. David Clarke
Rebecca and Johanna Thompson - the twins
Stephen Thompson

Other characters
Captain Scott Jones - Wagon Train Leader
David Clarke - now married to Eva Thompson
Rick Hughes and his nieces, Sarah and Carrie
Mrs. Long and her three daughters.

Freeman family - Pa, Ma, Sheila and her brother Joey

Bradley family - Pa and his daughter Gracie

Stan and his pregnant wife, Milly.

Mr Price and his son Almanzo

Mr. and Mrs. Newland

CHAPTER 1

⬥

OREGON TRAIL 1852

*R*ick Hughes answered Captain Jones' call to a meeting. As he walked toward the meeting point, he spotted Johanna Thompson up ahead. She was with her parents.

Even in a crowd of people, she stood out like a beacon. His gaze fell on her lips. He wondered what it would be like to kiss her. He shook off the thought as soon as it came into his head but there was no denying he had thought about it. Sadie wasn't dead a month and he had made her a promise to get the girls to Oregon where their father might be waiting for his family. He didn't have time to court a woman. Not any woman. Johanna was different. Her family had been helping him from the moment he had lost Sadie and the boys. One or another of the girls always sent over food to their fireside. Johanna often helped Sarah build up their fire and showed her how to prepare simple meals.

She was a wonderful cook and the children felt better now that they were eating proper food rather than the beans he had been preparing. He occasionally had time to cook meat but not often as driving the wagon, making repairs and taking his turn on guard duty meant he had little time left over. If only he was in a position to ask her father to court her. But how could he? With his future prospects thrown into confusion by Sadie's death, he had nothing concrete to offer anyone let alone someone as special as Johanna Thompson. Captain Jones' voice intruded on his thoughts.

"I called you all together to discuss the events of the last few days." Captain Jones reviewed the group of travelers sternly. "I asked Mr. and Mrs. Clarke to take a walk and leave us alone. I do not believe they need to hear what I have to say."

Johanna looked at her pa. He looked uncomfortable but he wasn't the only one.

"I have never come across such shameful behavior as we recently witnessed. If it wasn't for Mrs. Long, Mrs. Thompson, and her brave daughter, Johanna, David Clarke could very well be dead and buried." Captain Jones looked at each member of the assembled group.

Few returned his gaze. "Killed by a group of fellow travelers who didn't engage the brains they were born with."

Johanna glanced around the group and found a lot of expressions of shame. It looked like Captain Jones' words had hit home.

"Should anything happen to me, I would put David Clarke in charge of this group. He has shown himself to be brave, daring, resourceful and kind," Captain Jones continued, before one of the men spoke.

"Now see here, Jones. We didn't know he wasn't guilty. We are not responsible."

"Yes, you are, Mr. Price. You didn't know the facts, yet you were prepared to hang an innocent man for a murder he didn't commit. If I had my way, I would leave each and every one of you to fend for yourselves." As the group murmured in response, Captain Jones continued. "I promised to get as many of you to Oregon as safely as I could. I will keep that promise but if anyone ever behaves like this again, they are out. Do I make myself clear?"

Everyone nodded.

"Any questions?" Captain Jones barked.

Johanna waited to see who was brave enough to risk asking a question.

"Captain Jones, do you know what happened to

Chapman's other friend? I think his name was Bill?" Mr. Freeman asked.

"He snuck off in the night. Hopefully, we will never see him again. He is a wanted man. Captain Wilson said he is believed to be responsible for a number of crimes from bank robbery to kidnapping," Captain Jones replied.

"Good riddance. Can't have people like that around decent folks," Pa commented. "Has Captain Wilson taken Harold and Simon back to Fort Laramie? What was he doing so far away from his fort anyway. I mean it was lucky he was, but how on earth did Becky find him?"

"It was sheer luck. Captain Wilson was out on a long patrol. There have been reports of an Indian war between two of the tribes. So far, the caravans have been lucky. They haven't been dragged into the war but with two groups on the war path it is only a matter of time. Captain Wilson will take Chapman and his friend back to Fort Laramie where they will wait for a Justice of the Peace to come. That's if they make it there. The Captain will have no problem shooting them if they make life difficult for his men."

"What of Harold's wagon? He still has plenty of goods he was going to sell in Oregon. It would be a pity to leave them here," Mr. Bradley commented.

"I vote we give them to David Clarke. He deserves recognition of his service to the Long family. We accused and very nearly hanged an innocent man," Rick Hughes suggested.

Johanna was pleased to see Rick standing up for David.

"I played a big role in that," Pa murmured.

"Yes, you did and you should be ashamed of yourself." Ma's voice shook as she found it difficult to control her emotions. The events of the last forty-eight hours had taken their toll on everyone. Johanna had only realized how much danger she and Becky had been in when Eva explained why she had ignored her attempts to stop the wedding to Chapman.

"Who will drive the Long wagon now?" Mr. Freeman asked.

"One of my men has volunteered to do it. Mrs. Long has proved herself capable but the terrain we are coming to in the mountains is by far more difficult than anything we have covered to date. She will need more help and Jessie is one of the best men I know. The lack of men means we will have to double up on some shifts for guard duty. I expect no complaints."

There were none and the rest of the group went back to their wagons leaving Captain Jones, Mr. Hughes, Johanna and Becky.

"Captain Jones, I think everyone has learned their lesson. I don't expect anyone will cause trouble again," Becky said obviously not including herself in the same category as the rest of the crowd.

Johanna groaned at the look on the captain's face as Jones turned his full attention on Becky.

"Miss Thompson, you have single handedly caused more problems than the rest of the group put together."

"Pardon?" Becky's indignant response did nothing but fan the flames of Captain Jones' temper.

Johanna risked a look at Rick Hughes. He looked as if he was trying not to laugh.

"Where I come from, young ladies do not go gallivanting off into the night wearing a man's attire. They stay with their families," Captain Jones almost roared. Then probably realizing his words were carrying around the camp site, he lowered his tone. "While I understand your motives were pure, by acting in such a foolhardy way, you caused distress to your family and the rest of your companions."

"I was wearing a dress when I left," Becky protested.

"But your actions meant you lost that dress, did you not? You had to borrow some clothes from a solider after appearing in their midst half dressed. Do you have any idea of the danger you put yourself into? You behaved like a willful, disobedient child. If I was your father, I would put you over my knee and give you the spanking you deserve."

"Well, I..." Becky gave up trying to speak.

Johanna hid a smile although her ears were ringing on her sister's behalf. It was rare for Becky to be left speechless.

"Kindly remember, Miss Thompson, while I am not your father, I am in charge of this wagon train. I will not tolerate any more of your impulsive behavior. Please behave more like your sisters and less like a hoyden."

Becky didn't get a chance to answer as Captain Jones marched off. After a couple of seconds, Rick turned away to follow him.

CHAPTER 2

*J*ohanna put her arm around Becky's shoulders as her sister burst into tears. Her twin had been very brave, but her actions had also been extremely impulsive and fool-hardy. She guessed that although Captain Jones had said a lot of things, the one that hurt Becky the most was the fact he'd called her an impulsive child.

"I suppose you think he was right too?" Becky asked as her sobs subsided.

"I know why you did what you did. I think you were very brave,"Johanna said and gave her sister a hug "but it was dangerous. Captain Jones is right to have been concerned."

"He called me a child."

"He was angry."

"I know that but still he sees me as a child." Becky shuddered, one last sob escaping before she squared her shoulders. "He'll see. I am going to show him how much of a woman I am. That will teach him to speak to me like that."

Johanna didn't say anything but she couldn't help but pity Captain Jones a little. He really had no idea what he had let himself in for with her sister. It was obvious his anger came from his affection for her. Trust Becky not to spot that. She watched Becky as she walked back toward their parents' wagon. She didn't think for a minute the fireworks were over.

* * *

RICK WAITED for her to finish comforting her sister. He didn't want to interrupt them but he also had to tell her something. He had waited long enough.

He compared the girls as he waited. He had heard all about Becky's exploits–her helping to break David Clarke out and the subsequent events that lead to Becky returning dressed as a solider. He could understand why Captain Jones was annoyed, but he also thought it was a bit unfair to give her such a dressing down. The girl had guts. He wondered if there was something more personal between her and Jones, although he had yet to see any evidence of them courting. But Jones had behaved like he cared. Becky's reaction to his tirade suggested she returned his feelings. But what was he doing examining their relationship? His interest lay with her sister. While Becky was impetuous and impulsive, Johanna was steadier. Becky may be the more physically striking of the twins, but Rick was attracted to Johanna's inner spirit. Her quiet beauty struck a chord deep inside him.

He guessed her hair was lighter than it used to be, the continuous exposure to the sun turning it almost silver in some lights. The slight tanned glow on her face made her blue eyes look even bigger, but his gaze was attracted to her light pink lips. He ached to touch them with his own. To hold her in his arms, to tell her how he felt. But how did he feel? He was very attracted to her physically but it was more than that. He admired her courage, how she stood up to the people on the train like Price over the Indian issue. She was brave and while not fearless, as that would imply stupidity given the conditions they were traveling under, she kept her fears under control. She didn't whine either like some of the other women. Mrs. Newland would win the annual prize for whining.

She was patient with his nieces but firm when they needed to be disciplined. She expected them to behave and amazingly they did. Most of the children behaved better for Jo—as they called her—than they did for their own parents. Yet he hadn't heard her ever threaten them with a whipping or a slap. If they did something she disapproved of, she excluded them from their next activity. Children hated being ignored so her system, although simple, worked. He wondered how well it would work in the classroom. Back East, parents expected their children to be disciplined and therefore encouraged corporal punishment. How would Miss Thompson fare if she did become a school teacher and the board of the school insisted on corporal punishment? He had a feeling she was more likely to turn a whip on them than to touch a child.

She was as stubborn as she was brave which could prove a handicap in a wife. If he was to become a school teacher and made Johanna his wife, she would have a certain position to maintain in their local community. She couldn't be as forward in her opinions as she had been on the train. Why not? Isn't that what he admired? It was one thing for him to admire it, and it was another if her actions impeded his career. He wasn't looking to take her back East to earn the frowns of Boston society. Out West things were changing. He and Johanna could make those changes happen, together.

He had been so caught up in his thoughts, he didn't

realize he was staring at Johanna. She was alone and looking at him with a quizzical expression on her face.

"I'm sorry. I didn't want to interrupt your moment with your sister, but I was hoping to speak with you."

"Yes?" Johanna's soft voice set his heart racing. Was he wrong to hope his interest in her was reflected in her eyes?

"I just wanted you to know I am sorry I didn't come to Clarke's aid earlier. I was on guard duty that evening and missed everything."

"That's quite all right."

"I don't know Clarke well but he seems like a fine chap." Seriously, could he sound any more condescending? But his brain refused to engage, her smile chasing away all his thoughts but the wish to take her in his arms and kiss her senseless. He shuffled uncomfortably. "Anyway, I just wanted you to know."

"Thank you, Mr. Hughes," Johanna said, smiling but with a curious expression in her eyes. As if she was waiting for something. Maybe he could ask if he could speak to her father. Before he got a chance to speak, her younger brother appeared calling her name.

"Johanna, Ma wants to know if you have forgotten the dishes."

"I am so sorry, Mr. Hughes. I best get back."

And then she was gone.

CHAPTER 3

"We will make camp here tonight. Tomorrow we cross the river," Captain Jones said as he surveyed the group. "There is no ferry so we will drive across. The current isn't strong nor is it too deep. You will all need to raise the wagons to prevent their contents getting wet."

Johanna watched the men working. They had cut some willow saplings and used them to raise the wagon beds about six inches, hoping it would be high enough to stop the water from ruining their supplies. Ma had them wrapping everything in extra covers just in case. She was thankful this would be their last time crossing the Sweetwater River.

She listened to the evening sounds around the camp. The men pounded the tent pegs into the ground while the women scraped the dinner dishes clean. Someone was playing the fiddle while the children laughed and ran around the various campfires. They had made so many friends among the other families traveling with them. It would be hard to split from them when they finally arrived in Oregon.

Later that evening, her parents sat around their campfire for longer than usual. Becky was working on her sewing so Johanna took out the small quilting piece she was completing for Carrie. The little girl wanted a blanket for her doll.

"I was speaking to Gracie for quite a while today. She has some grand plans for Oregon," Ma commented without looking up from her work.

"What does she want to do?" Becky asked.

"She and Joey plan on claiming six hundred and forty acres of land once they marry. They are going to have the best farm in the area. She is going to have the prettiest house and garden."

"You sound like you disapprove, Ma?" Johanna knew it wasn't in her ma's nature to put someone else's dreams down.

"I don't disapprove but I am concerned. The poor girl has herself convinced everything will be perfect. Real life isn't like that. It is going to be hard work."

"She knows that, Della, she is just being optimistic about the opportunities ahead of all of us."

"I think it's more than that, Paddy. She has the idea she has to be the perfect wife too. A bit like our Eva."

"What's wrong with Eva?" Pa's voice bristled.

"Don't speak to me using that tone. There is nothing wrong with our daughter apart from the fact she seems intent on working herself into the ground. Since she got married, she has insisted on doing all their cooking and chores herself. She won't take any help."

"It has only been a few days. She just wants to show Clarke what a treasure she is."

"David Clarke knows that more than most. He is as concerned as I am. He asked her to let them take their meals here. He mentioned I could do with some extra help but she won't listen. She thinks he is insulting her. I fear they had their first row about it."

"You better be careful, Della. You didn't take kindly to my mam getting involved in our business." Pa laughed as if remembering the early days of his marriage.

"Maybe at first but I learned your mother was usually right."

"I will speak to Eva, Ma. I can ask her to help us to ease your burden."

"Thank you, Johanna."

"So what plans do my girls have for their lives in Oregon?"

Becky excused herself quickly leaving Johanna to answer her father.

"My dream is the same as it always was, Pa."

"To be surrounded by children. You have certainly got plenty of practice on this trip." Pa beamed at her. "You will make a fine mother and wife."

"I want to be a school teacher, Pa."

"Not that again. I thought you would forget about teaching. It is not a career for a woman."

"How can you say that? A lot of teachers are female."

"Dried up old spinsters. Not fresh faced beautiful girls who can make a fine match."

"Pa, I am not one of your prized animals. I am a person with my own thoughts and dreams," she protested. But her disrespectful tone got her into trouble with her ma.

"Johanna Thompson, mind your tone. Do not speak to your father like that."

"Sorry, Ma. I best get to bed. It's late."

Johanna had to leave for fear she would say something else. She was determined to be a school teacher whether her pa agreed or not.

CHAPTER 4

*T*he next morning, Johanna waited by the shore. Milly walked up behind her, her hand lying on her stomach protectively.

"It won't be like last time, will it?" Milly's nervous tone was matched by the look in her eyes.

"No, of course not. Look, it's barely deep enough to swim in. We will all be fine," Johanna said hoping she sounded sincere. She didn't like river crossings any more than Milly did. "How are you feeling?"

Milly blushed. "Better now the sickness has passed over. Your ma has been wonderful. It helps having someone who understands what it's like," Milly said quietly. "She makes it seem less scary."

"Listen to Ma and you will be fine."

"She promised to help Stan look after the baby if

anything was to happen." Milly bit her lip staring at the river.

"Nothing bad is going to happen, Milly. You'll see. God willing, we will be in Oregon before your little one makes an appearance."

Johanna crossed her fingers as the hope shone out of the other girl's eyes. She hoped she was right. Having your first baby was bad enough, but out here in the wilds? But Indian women do it all the time. That was different though. They were used to it.

She turned her gaze back to the happenings at the water. She bit her lip watching everyone's progress, in particular her ma and pa's wagon, David's, and not least of all Rick and the girls. She was riding Pa's horse across as he wanted to take the wagon.

Thankfully, everyone crossed without incident and they camped about half a mile from the river. The grass was better than they had seen for some days. Captain Jones was concerned about the oxen losing their strength so he wanted to take advantage of every good grazing opportunity that came their way. She spotted Eva looking a little strained and very tired. She made a mental note to speak to her alone the first chance she got.

Later she saw Eva moving toward the river presumably to get some water so she followed her.

"How is married life?" Johanna teased her older sister.

Eva blushed prettily. "It's wonderful, although I can't wait until we have our own home and some privacy."

"Is that what this is all about?" Johanna asked.

"What do you mean?"

Johanna knew she had to tread carefully or risk hurting her sister's feelings.

"I mean you setting up your own fire and cooking your meals. Why don't you and David just eat with us? It would be less work for you, and David would feel better not leaving you alone so much."

"Has he said something?" Eva's eyes filled with concern.

"Of course not, but I know he worries about you when he is on guard duty. You don't have anything to prove, Eva."

"I am a married woman now with responsibilities."

"Your main responsibility is to keep both of you as healthy as possible. The hard work won't stop when we get to Oregon." Her sister had that stubborn look she sometimes got in her eyes. "Eva, please. I need you at our fireside. You know what Pa is like. He thinks Becky and I are still children."

Eva's eyes blazed with curiosity now. "Is this about

the man you were dancing with at the wedding? Isn't his name Hughes?"

Johanna wished she had left Eva to it now. One sister knowing about her love life was bad enough, but two?

"I was dancing with Mr. Hughes but that's not what this is about. I want to be a school teacher when I get to Oregon. Pa thinks I am too young to know what I want. Even though he got married and everything by our age."

"He's a man."

"That shouldn't make a difference." Surprised at her sister's traditional response, Johanna's tone was sharper than she'd intended. She immediately softened it again. It wouldn't do to get on Eva's bad side. "Please, Eva. He listens to you."

"You mean he is being nice to me because of what happened with Harold," Eva said sadly.

Johanna knew it still hurt that their pa had favored Harold over David so obviously, but in time, that wound would heal. "Well, that too. But he does listen to you, Eva, you are his first born and hold a special place in his heart. Don't protest. I am not complaining. I heard him tell Ma you reminded him of Granny."

"I wish Granny had been at the wedding. She loves David."

"You will have to write to her and tell her all about it. You would have time to write letters if you came back to our fire. Will you, please? It makes more sense if we share the chores. You will wear yourself out at this rate."

"I will speak to my husband." Eva's teasing tone gave Johanna hope. If anyone could talk their pa round, it was Eva.

Johanna gave her sister a hug. "Thanks, Eva."

* * *

As Johanna wandered back to camp, she couldn't stop thinking about Rick Hughes. He wasn't as tall as her father or as well built. He looked rather like a school teacher instead of a farmer. His dark hair and slightly sallow colored skin made his eyes look even darker. He didn't shave regularly but she didn't mind. In fact, the light stubble across his chin made him look older and more distinguished in her mind at least. It was obvious from speaking with him, he was well educated. His cultured accent and excellent general knowledge spoke of a well-funded education. He wouldn't be at all out of place in society parlor, although they may make him take off his dusty shoes. She giggled at the image of him standing in front of society's most impervious matrons, all dusty and smelling distinctly of horse. She wondered why he was heading out West. He looked as if he should have gone in the opposite direction.

CHAPTER 5

"Johanna, is that snow on top of the hills? I said it was but Stephen said it wasn't. He said it was stones."

"I think you are right, Carrie, looks like snow to me."

"Can we go see?"

Johanna smiled. "No, sweetheart, we can't. Those hills look close, but in reality, they are far away. We would get lost."

"So how do I prove to Stephen he's wrong?"

"Tell my brother girls are always right."

Carrie's face lit up as she ran after Stephen. Johanna heard her telling him how boys were wrong about everything. Her brother was arguing back.

She pulled her woolen shawl around her as she gathered more fuel for the fire. There was a cool sharp breeze blowing making her believe it was snow. She hadn't told Carrie two men from the wagon train had placed a rather large bet and were now in the process of finding out who was right. She didn't understand them betting over silly things. Nobody in the wagon train was very poor but still they didn't have money to waste either. They were a long way from Oregon.

"Who upset you?"

She twirled around at the sound of Rick's voice. She hadn't noticed him ride up. He must have been out hunting, although he didn't seem to have caught anything.

"Nobody. I was just thinking," she said quickly, her heart racing at his closeness.

"Your face was all screwed up like this." He made a face making her laugh.

"I was thinking about the men who had gambled on whether the snow was granite or not. It seems a silly waste of time and money," Johanna answered as soon as she stopped laughing.

"I guess but the trail is rather boring and monotonous. If anything helps to pass the time, providing it doesn't hurt anyone, I think it's fine."

"They could read a book. It is safer and cheaper."

He laughed. "True, Miss School Teacher, but how many of these men can read? I figure most of our company are illiterate or barely know enough to get by. Not much chance of schooling for many of these men."

Johanna flushed. She had been insensitive, something very unusual for her. Usually she was the one pointing out the obvious reasons to her sisters. Why did this man always make her feel as she should be apologizing?

"Have you seen the girls?"

"Carrie is off teasing Stephen and Sarah was with Becky and Ma earlier. I think Becky took her to visit her friend Milly. She won't have left her alone, don't worry."

"I don't know what I would do without you and your family, Miss Thompson. Thank goodness we joined this wagon train at Fort Kearney and not another one."

Johanna's cheeks went redder. Flustered, she turned back to collecting fuel too quickly. Her foot caught in her skirt and she fell over. She was so embarrassed at being sprawled over the ground, she didn't realize how much leg she was showing. As soon as she did, she clambered to get up but after trying to put weight on her foot, she screeched and fell down once again.

*　*　*

He was by her side in an instant feeling guilty for distracting her and contributing to her fall.

"Is it broken?"

She was very pale and breathing quickly. Her eyes were shimmering but as yet she hadn't cried. "I don't think so," she whispered. "I will be fine in a minute."

"Let me be the judge of that. I am going to take off your boot."

She jerked back. "You can't do that. It's not seemly."

"I don't care." He took off her boot and whipped off her stocking before she could get her breath back. Her ankle was already starting to swell, all red and puffy. He felt around the bone gingerly not wanting to hurt her even more. "I don't think its broken but it looks like a bad sprain. I won't put your boot back on as I don't think you will get it off again." As he spoke he rolled her stocking into her boot. "I will take you to your ma."

She looked at him and the horse. "How?"

"You can ride in front of me. Spirit won't mind, will you boy?"

The horse butted his shoulder gently as if answering.

"Can you help me please? I don't think I can stand up."

He lifted her as easily as if she was a bag of sugar before placing her gently on the horse. He pulled her closer to him.

"Do you feel dizzy?"

She nodded.

"Lay your head back against me. Close your eyes and don't panic. I will ride slowly."

She closed her eyes as she lay back against his chest, conscious of the strength of his body. Her foot ached horribly but it was almost worth it to get so close to him. She glanced at his strong hands, rough from hard work yet they had felt so gentle when he tended her ankle. Her heart was fluttering remembering the look of concern in his eyes. Was it her imagination or had he just kissed her hair? She closed her eyes, letting herself relax into the circle of his arms.

Unfortunately, it didn't take long to get back to camp. He helped her down from the horse as her ma fussed around her. As he released her, she felt bereft. She wanted to cry not just from the pain in her ankle.

"I don't think it is broken, Mrs. Thompson, but it probably should be strapped. Miss Thompson should rest as much as possible."

"Thank you, Mr. Hughes, for coming to her assistance. We are very grateful," Ma responded as she waited for him to leave. Johanna knew her mother wasn't going to examine her ankle in front of a strange man.

"Least I could do given what your family has done for my girls. Take care, Miss Thompson." He turned to go back to Spirit.

"Thank you, Mr. Hughes." Johanna finally found her voice. He smiled at her and for a minute she forgot the throbbing pain.

"You are mighty flushed, young lady. I wonder if it isn't broken. Let me have a proper look at it."

Johanna winced as her ma examined her. She agreed it wasn't fractured.

"The swelling suggests a bad sprain. You will be traveling in the wagon for the next few days."

"Yes, Ma."

CHAPTER 6

The next few days passed by so slowly. Johanna was going out of her mind with boredom. She sewed and crocheted but the hours still passed so slowly. Her pa took pity on her one evening and carried her to sit by the fire.

"Looks like Captain Jones is right. Those sky's hint at stormy weather coming our way. I best go check the cattle. You all right alone or do you want me to fetch your ma?"

"I am fine, thanks, Pa."

"Your ma and Becky are over with the Freemans. She won't be much longer. I best get to it."

Johanna stared into the flames trying not to think of the storms coming their way. Ever since she'd been little, she'd hated lightning. The noise of thunder didn't bother her much. She was still deep in thought when Rick Hughes walked by.

"Good evening, Miss Thompson, I hope your ankle is improving?"

"Yes, thank you. Ma reckons I should be able to walk on it in a day or so."

"I have something I've been meaning to give you. I got it from a friend back East. I thought you might enjoy it." He looked at her shyly handing her a package. "It might break the monotony of traveling in the wagon."

"What is it?"

"Open it and see."

She opened the package realizing it held a book. Looking at the cover she gasped. "*Oliver Twist*. I've been dying to read this. Have you read it? Are you sure you want to lend it to me?"

"Yes, and yes," he smiled.

"Oh, thank you. This will help, especially tonight."

"Why tonight?"

She read the curiosity in his gaze. "Sorry, I didn't mean to whine. I don't like storms."

"Oh that. I don't think any of us do. Speaking of which, come on I will see you back to your wagon. You best get in before the rains start. I don't want to be responsible for you catching a chill as well as a sore ankle."

"You didn't make me fall."

"I was rather hoping I distracted you a little."

Johanna didn't know what to say to the intense look in his eyes. For once she wished she was as accomplished a flirt as Becky. Her twin wouldn't sit there gawping at the man she liked, opening and closing her mouth like a fish.

"Thank you for the lend of the book," she finally managed to stammer.

"It's a gift, Jo."

Startled by his familiarity, she glanced up at him.

"Sorry, I apologize. Miss Thompson."

"I like Jo but I don't think my pa will let me accept a gift." She couldn't look at him for fear he would see her feelings in her eyes.

"Tell him it's payment then for you looking after the girls."

He helped her to her feet, his arm remaining around her waist. She knew she should say goodnight but she didn't want him to leave. Yet by staying she risked her pa coming over to ask him what his intentions were.

"Thank you. I will treasure it."

"I rather think it will make you cry, so please don't hate me."

"I could never do that," she said softly looking up into his face.

Before she knew what was happening, he kissed her quickly, his lips barely brushing hers before walking back toward his wagon.

"That you, Johanna?"

"Yes, Pa," she called back hoping her pa wouldn't come too near. He'd see her all flushed.

"Go to bed, girl. We got an early start tomorrow."

"Yes, Pa, goodnight." She got dressed for bed, thankful her twin was already asleep. She felt her lips with her finger. Had he really kissed her or had she just imagined it?

* * *

THE KISS, although brief, had proved her lips were just as delicious as he had imagined. There was a spark between them that threatened to engulf his entire body. He had taken a risk kissing her like that. Thankfully, his restraint had kicked in preventing him from sweeping her into his arms and deepening the kiss. Her father could have returned any second.

As Rick neared his wagon, he heard his niece crying. Waves of guilt threatened to overwhelm him. He should never have let Sadie talk him into the trip out West. She wasn't strong enough to travel, the last difficult birth leaving her weak. But only in body. When Sadie set her mind to something, nobody could change it. But he was the man of the house. He should have put his foot down. If he had, his sister and maybe the boys would still be alive.

What would Sadie have made of Johanna Thompson? Would they have been friends? Somehow, he thought they might have been. He didn't know Miss Thompson well but she seemed to share their values. The way she had stood up for her belief that all people were equal had impressed him. She had a quiet nature but when provoked was almost as fiery as her other sisters.

CHAPTER 7

"What did you do today, girls?"

"Jo, that's what we call Johanna now, showed us how to crochet. She is going to make a new dress for my doll. Isn't that nice of her?" Carrie said climbing onto Rick's lap. She had taken to doing that since losing her ma. She twirled her finger in his hair reminding him he needed a haircut.

"She is very nice doing that. What about you, Sarah, what did you do?"

"Nothing."

"Really?" He knew Sarah was upset about something, not just from her tone but also the look on her face.

"Come here, sweetheart. What's wrong?"

"Nothing."

"Is that all you can say tonight?" When Sarah kicked at a pebble in response, Rick asked Carrie. "What upset your sister?"

"I don't know. She's been real grumpy all day."

"Have not."

"Have too."

"Stop it, girls. Carrie run along to bed and let me speak to Sarah, please." At the mutinous look on Carrie's face, he said "Please. I will come in and read you a story in a minute."

Carrie climbed down from his knee and walked slowly to the wagon. Rick waited until she was inside before gesturing for Sarah to come sit beside him.

"Can you tell me what's wrong?"

"I'm scared."

Rick's chest tightened. "Who scared you, Sarah?"

"You did."

"Me?"

"I heard you talking to someone. You said you were thinking of going back home."

Rick could have kicked himself for not checking that he didn't have an audience when he had spoken to Mr. Bradley about his plans. They had discussed whether it was wiser taking the children back or moving forward. The consensus was it was probably safer to continue with the wagon train than to try to return on their own. He wondered how long Sarah had been listening?

"I don't want to go home. There is nobody there now. We have to go to Oregon. Pa is waiting for us. Isn't he?"

Rick watched the fire for a couple of seconds trying to work out what to say. Hopefully, their pa was waiting, but there had been no news since that first letter. The lack of letters had been part of the reason his sister had wanted to make the journey. She'd had a funny feeling all was not well. But how could he say that to his ten-year-old niece? She had just lost her ma.

"I thought it would be easier to go back. The route ahead is dangerous and I am not much good with girls. I never had kids and until I stayed with your ma, I hadn't spent that much time around them."

"But I can manage. I know I don't cook too good but I can learn. Jo can teach me."

"Sarah, honey, you are only ten years old. You can't take on all the chores."

"I can if it means we can find Pa. That's if he is still..."

"Still what?" Rick's heart raced. What did Sarah know of her pa? "Sarah, tell me what you meant?"

"Ma was talking a lot just before she died. She told Benjy that he had to be head of the family as Pa might be dead. She was crying and asked Benjy not to tell us. But he didn't get a chance did he, 'cause he died too. Him, Ma and baby George. Why did they have to die?"

The tears came thick and fast. All he could do was cuddle her. He didn't know what to say to make her feel better. How could you explain death to a child? It was just something that happened.

"Sarah, your ma is up in Heaven now looking down on you. She is real proud of the way you look after Carrie."

"She can't be. If she was here, she would give me a clip around the ear for shouting at Carrie."

"No, she wouldn't. She knows all sisters fight. But she might want you to be a little more caring with your sister. She is younger and probably more scared than you are. You are all she has left of her family now."

Sarah pushed him away. "Are you leaving us as well? What about Pa? Is he dead?"

"Sarah, shush, Carrie will hear you."

"Well, is he?"

Rick wondered if he should lie but something in Sarah's face told him that would be a mistake.

"I won't leave you, Sarah. I promised your ma I would take you to Oregon to find your pa, and that's what I will do."

"What if he is dead?"

"We will deal with that at the time. I hope he isn't. You know that the post doesn't work properly."

"But there should have been at least one letter?"

Rick nodded not wanting to make her hope dissolve with any words. "Come here, darling. I promise you won't be alone. I will always be with you."

"Will you be our Pa if our real one is...d... gone?" she asked, her voice slipping on the last word.

Rick looked into her eyes, saw the uncertainty and fear. He knew he had to do something, say something to ease that. But promise to be their pa? That wasn't in his plans. At twenty-three it wasn't in most men's plans. He wanted to start a school and teach children and maybe adults too. He had intended on setting up a string of schools. The current lack of education was a serious issue out West. But how could he drag two young girls with him. How could he leave them either? He didn't know if their father had any family. He couldn't remember Ellis mentioning any. He took too long to answer her.

"You don't want us either." Sarah ran to the wagon. He called to her to stop but she ignored him.

Darnation, but he had made a mess of that too.

* * *

THE NEXT MORNING Sarah wouldn't speak to him. No matter what he said or did, she continued to ignore him. Carrie said she was being grumpy but he knew his niece was hurting and it was all his fault. They had arranged to go walking with Johanna again. Maybe being with Miss Thompson would help Sarah feel a bit better.

CHAPTER 8

*J*ohanna was so confused. Rick seemed to like her but there were days it was as if he couldn't get away from her fast enough. The other day, his hand brushed hers and it had lingered on the small of her back longer than necessary when he ushered her around a group of excited children. He had smiled at her too, making her feel like the only girl in the world. Then today, he was almost rude in his haste to get away from her. It was so frustrating. She longed to ask him straight out but her ma would have a fit. She had drummed it into all her girls often enough that the man always made the first move.

She picked up the dress she was crocheting for Carrie's doll. It should be finished by now but she couldn't concentrate on it. Carrie was behaving as normal but Sarah had closed up like a book. She was really worried about the young girl. She wasn't eating properly. It was as if she had given up on happiness. She never smiled and rarely talked. Carrie had said she was sulky but Johanna knew it had to be more than just that. She had tried talking to the young girl but failed to get a response. She had to speak to Rick about it, tell him her worries. Are you doing this for the child or yourself? She couldn't answer her own thoughts truthfully.

Rick had provided meat earlier in the week. She went back to the girls' wagon and had the fire lit and the stew warming with biscuits on the side by the time Rick came back to the wagon. She waited as he saw to his horse. He looked tired, the lines etched around his eyes more visible as the white marks stood out against his tanned face. He couldn't be getting much rest with driving the wagon all day and then having to catch meat as well as show up for guard duty. It was a lot for one person. Add in two young girls and it was easy to see why he was shattered.

"Miss Thompson, thank you for waiting with the girls but you didn't have to."

"I did. I have something to ask you. It will wait until after dinner," she said sending a quick glance in Sarah's direction in the hope he would know she wanted to speak privately. "If you want to wash up, the girls made some stew and biscuits for you."

"Makes a nice change from beans. Thank you kindly, ladies." Carrie laughed as he swept his hat off his head and bowed to all of them. Sarah barely looked at him never mind smiled.

Something must have happened between Rick and Sarah. Johanna was determined not to go back to her own wagon until she got things straightened out.

"Are you joining us for dinner?" Rick asked as he took his place near the fire.

Johanna was about to say her ma would have some waiting for her but Carrie answered on her behalf.

"Course she's staying. She likes us."

"Guess I am staying then," Johanna agreed as she took a seat and began dishing up their meal. Sarah gave out cups of water. As Johanna gave everyone a plate, she saw Sarah listlessly pick at hers.

"Don't you like stew, Sarah?"

"She likes it just fine. She's just sulking."

Ricks tone surprised Johanna. Usually he had lots of patience with the girls, but not tonight. She saw the tears in Sarah's eyes and longed to give her a cuddle. She was too young to have been through the devastation of losing her ma and brothers. She tried again. "Sarah, sweetheart, are you feeling all right?"

Sarah turned her big blue eyes on Johanna who held her breath at the look of loss and confusion on her face. "Sweetheart, if you are feeling ill you need to tell us so we can make you better."

"She's fine."

Johanna whirled on Rick. "I didn't ask you. She obviously isn't fine."

She took the plate from Sarah and led the girl to the wagon. "You stay here and let me deal with your uncle."

"You will make him angry."

"Not as angry as he has made me. Go on inside and lie down. Everything is going to be all right."

"I know you mean that, Jo, but you couldn't be more wrong. Uncle Rick doesn't want us. Pa is dead, so when we get to Oregon he is going to dump us somewhere. It will just be me and Carrie."

The girl's shuddering sobs racked her whole body and fed Johanna's anger until she thought she was going to blow off steam like a boiling kettle. "Come on, darling, you got it all wrong. Your uncle Rick wouldn't do that. He loves you. Carrie too. I know you miss your ma. You have every right to be upset. But don't make up stories. It's not nice."

Sarah turned on her. "I am not lying. You go ask him for yourself."

"Ask me what?" Rick was standing in front of them at the opening of the wagon canvas.

Johanna had no idea how long he had been there. Would he be angry with her for interfering? But then what did it matter? A child was hurting and she needed to help.

"Sarah thinks her pa is dead and once you get to Oregon you will be leaving her and Carrie there. Alone. Of course I told her she must be mistaken. You wouldn't do that."

The few seconds of silence told Johanna the child had spoken the truth. She put a hand to her mouth to stop herself from saying something she'd regret. She turned toward Sarah. "I apologize for not believing you, darling. I'm sorry. We will talk tomorrow."

Trying to hold her temper in, she climbed down from the wagon. Her long skirt made it awkward but she brushed aside his attempt to help. "Don't touch me," she hissed at him, trying to keep her voice down.

"Miss Thompson, it's not like it sounds. I can't... I mean it's not... Oh, I don't have to explain myself to you anyway."

"No you don't. But I hope you can live with yourself. You are a grown man and all those two girls have. I never thought I would ever say this to you, but you must be the most selfish, self-centered individual I have ever had the misfortune to meet."

"Jo, don't say that, please. Let me explain."

She stood for a second looking into his face. He looked the same as he had earlier before her vision of him being the perfect man shattered before her very eyes.

"Go on then... I'm waiting."

hat could he say? How could he possibly explain to this woman with a heart of gold that he wasn't ready to take on two young girls. He didn't know exactly what he would do in Oregon. Sure, he had a dream to set up a number of schools but what if it wasn't that easy? What if parents couldn't afford to send their children to school? How would he look after two young'uns when he planned to be traveling from one area to the next?

"I don't have all night."

Her words, or rather her tone, brought him back to reality. He looked at her and immediately wished he hadn't. Her eyes were full of anger, loathing but also hurt. He had hurt her as he had Sarah.

He twisted his hands together.

"I don't know what happened to Sarah's pa. My sister believed something bad happened and that's why he stopped writing."

"You mean they are orphans."

"I don't know for sure but yes, probably."

"Oh the poor girls. They need you more than ever now."

"Jo, I am only twenty-three. What do I know about raising two young'uns?"

"You can learn. It's not hard. It is much more important for them to be with someone they know and love than it is for them to be left to fend for themselves."

"I wouldn't do that," he spat, immediately contrite as she flinched at his tone. "Sorry, I didn't mean to snap. I would never leave them alone. I love those girls."

"So why are we having this conversation?"

She was beautiful when she was mad. This wasn't the time or place for him to even notice such a thing.

"I was planning on leaving them with an orphanage or mission. Somewhere like the Whitman Mission."

"Oh that's a good example." Her sarcastic tone hurt. "A lot of those kids died in the Indian attack."

"Wrong example but something similar."

"I don't think Oregon has been established long

enough to have a proper orphanage system. But even if it did, you couldn't be cruel enough to leave the girls there. Nobody will want to adopt a ten-year-old, particularly if Sarah insists on being surly. Carrie, with her sweet smile and loving nature will be snapped up and you will have achieved everything your sister never wanted. Most of her family dead and the remaining siblings having no contact." Tears made her voice tremble making him feel worse.

"What would you have me do?" He knew he was pleading but he genuinely wanted to know. He didn't like his plan either. If he was honest he hadn't given it proper thought.

"You keep them. Whatever plans you have you give up. You became their pa the day your sister gave them into your safekeeping. You can't go back on that now," she insisted.

"But what if I am no good for them? If I can't get a job they won't eat and could starve."

"Well, that is just about the most stupid thing I have ever heard. Why couldn't you get a job? You are well educated, thoughtful, kind, considerate, good with animals and people..." Johanna flushed, the pink glow on her cheeks making her eyes sparkle.

"I thought I was a selfish, self-important donkey."

"I was being cruel to the donkey," she retaliated, but he sensed she was more willing to listen to him now.

"Please sit down and have some coffee. I will do my best to explain my reasons." When she hesitated, he persisted. "It would be nice to get someone else's opinion, once they know the full story."

His last comment got her attention. She nodded. "Just let me settle Carrie in the wagon. You can make the coffee provided you don't burn it or make it too strong."

"No, ma'am"

Carrie was sleeping so instead he carried his niece to the wagon while Johanna made the coffee. He laid Carrie down gently by her sister. "Sarah, I promise I will try my best to sort this out for everyone."

His niece had her back to him and didn't even move at his words. He patted her shoulder but she moved closer to the canvas.

He climbed down to where Johanna sat waiting at the fire, her blonde hair glistening in the firelight. He was suddenly terrified of her reaction to what he had to say. It sounded so much more reasonable in his brain then when he had tried to explain it a few minutes earlier.

He didn't want to lose her respect or her admiration. He thought she must like him a little bit. He had caught her looking at him a couple of times but he had no right to make any romantic approach. Didn't he have enough problems with his two nieces? But he could solve everything if Johanna agreed to marry him. Where had that thought come from? Yet as he stood there watching her back, he realized he'd been thinking of her ever since they'd first met.

CHAPTER 10

ohanna felt his eyes on her. She waited for him to come toward her but he seemed to be waiting. She looked around, catching his gaze. The look in his eyes took her breath away. She had to break the connection yet found she couldn't. She summoned the anger she had felt toward him only moments before but even that had cooled somewhat. She sensed there was much more to the story than Sarah had told her. Suddenly, she wondered if she should be sitting there at all. It was late, they were alone, a single male not related to her family. If anyone should walk by, her reputation would be compromised. Even as the thought crossed her mind, she found she didn't care. All that mattered now was Rick.

She fought every impulse in her body. She wanted to move toward him, to ease the troubled expression from his face but she knew that wouldn't be the right thing to do. He had to make the next move. He had been forced into being a father. It was not right to try to persuade him to become a...husband. The word whispered across her mind mocking her. All those times her sisters had talked about getting married, settling down and having a family came flooding through her mind.

"Miss Thompson, thank you for waiting. I very much appreciate it."

She winced at his formal tone but stayed silent. It was time for him to explain. When he stayed silent, she gestured to the stone opposite hers.

"Why don't you sit down and tell me the story from the start? So I can understand."

"Sadie, my sister, married young against our pa's wishes. He didn't think Toby Ellis had what it took to be a family man. He had all these dreams yet no real work ethic. But Sadie was in love and when she threatened to elope, he gave his permission for them to wed. Pa gave them some acres of land, good land hoping that would be enough of an incentive for Ellis to get himself sorted out."

"But it wasn't?"

"At first it seemed to be. Sadie and Ellis were happy. Soon she was pregnant. Ellis was very much the proud father to be. He was pleased as punch when their first child, Benjamin or Benjy as he was known was born. Eleven months later, Sarah came along. Then another two babies both of whom died in the first few weeks."

"Oh, your poor sister. I can't imagine how heart-broken she must have been."

"I wasn't there so I didn't see her but I guess she was."

"Where were you?" Johanna gasped. She hadn't meant to be so forward. "I'm sorry, you must think me dreadfully nosy."

"No, it's fine. I was back East with my grandmother. I went to college. She had some grand plan to make me become a banker. But then Pa wrote..." He stopped to take a drink.

Johanna guessed he needed a couple of seconds to compose himself.

"Sadie was in trouble. Ellis had gone and the bank was threatening to foreclose."

"But I thought your pa gave them the land."

"He did, but Ellis had taken out a loan on it. He'd gambled it away and then ran leaving Sadie and the young'uns. Pa and me, we headed out, found him and brought him home. We gave them enough money to keep the bank happy. The balance was supposed to be paid when the next crops were brought in. Sadie was happy again, although I don't think she trusted him fully. Ellis disappeared again. He told her he was heading to Oregon to claim some land and start his own farm away from her interfering family. She found out she was pregnant some weeks after he left."

"But you don't believe him?"

The eyes that caught hers now were tortured. "When we found him that first time, he had another woman. That woman believed herself to be married. She was in the family way. Pa nearly killed Ellis. I almost wish he had. At the very least we should have left him where we found him. But Pa had made Sadie a promise to bring him home so that's what he did."

"And your pa?"

"When he found out Ellis had run out again and Sadie was pregnant, he couldn't handle it. He gave Sadie an ultimatum—to pack her bags and head back East with him to my grandmothers or he would cut his ties."

"Sadie chose her husband?"

Rick nodded. "I couldn't let her make this trip alone. She was determined to go to Oregon to find him. But...well, you know the rest of her story."

Johanna sniffed, trying to keep the well of tears

down. She rummaged for a handkerchief. He handed one to her. "It's clean."

"Why don't you bring the girls back to live in the east?"

"Pa died on his way back and my grandmother and Sadie never got along. She has a cruel streak reserved only for the women in the family. Pa was her favorite, but his sisters speak of a woman I have never seen. Sadie made me swear not to take the girls to their grandmother."

"So instead you want to dump them at an orphanage?"

"Jo!"

She jerked at his tone.

"Sorry, I shouldn't have shouted. I don't want to dump, as you so kindly put it, anyone anywhere. But I don't know how to be a farmer. How am I going to make enough money to keep the girls?"

"What were you going to do before Sadie died? Surely you weren't going to leave her in Oregon alone with the children."

"No, of course not. I was going to help her get set up and employ a man of labor to help her. I would call as often as I was able."

"Why couldn't you help her run the farm? Didn't she know enough to tell you want to do?"

"She did but I had other dreams. I still do. I want to teach Johanna. But not just in one place. I want to set up a string of schools all over the territory. So all children can access education. It's a basic right and it makes so much difference to their future. I am sure you agree given what you told me of your dreams?"

He looked so hopeful she was tempted for a second not to respond. But she couldn't just sit there and listen.

"I understand your need to see children in school. I agree education benefits everyone and helps give people a chance to escape poverty." She faltered at the look of hope and understanding in his eyes. "But no dream is worth sacrificing family over. Those girls are your flesh and blood. You are their only hope now. You cannot, you must not leave them to the mercy of an orphanage. They have been through enough, especially Sarah. She must know something of her father regardless of how hard your sister tried to keep it from her. Children pick up more than we give them credit. For her sake and Carrie's, I beg you please don't do this."

"You have a very tender heart, Miss Thompson."

"I believe you do as well. If you didn't you would have turned back that first day after burying your sister and her children. You would have put the girls on a train to your grandmother and gone back to living your dream but you didn't. Why not?"

"I couldn't do that. I couldn't break my word to my sister."

"And now?"

"What do you mean?

"Is it any easier to break your word now? Because that is exactly what you would be doing. Your sister trusted you with the most precious thing she had. Her children. Her little girls. Two gorgeous little people who deserve only the best things from life."

"I know but..."

"I don't think it's because of your dream Mr. Hughes. I think it's because deep down you're scared silly you won't cut it as a father." Johanna stood up. "Believe me if you leave these girls, then you will prove your fears right. No decent pa, whether by blood or by circumstance, would leave his girls to the mercy of strangers. Not while there was a breath left in his body. I thought you were a real man. Perhaps I was mistaken."

* * *

JOHANNA WALKED AWAY, praying he wouldn't follow her. She didn't want him to see her tears. Not only for the girls and his sister but for him as well. She knew he was scared. She could help him but only if he asked her to. If they were married, she could love the girls, look after them on a daily basis leaving him free to pursue his dream in a modified version. What of your dreams? She sighed. Her dreams were always just that. There was no way she could combine being a wife and mother with being a school teacher. It simply wasn't done.

CHAPTER 11

*J*ohanna avoided Rick and the girls. She couldn't face the devastation on young Sarah's face nor could she face Rick. She didn't want to accept he had made the decision to leave the girls even if his words suggested he had. There was another way. But he had to find that path alone.

"Why are we going this way, Pa?"

"The other route takes us over a river and Captain Jones said it would be difficult to ford it after all the rain. So we are taking the one crossing the hills. It will be hard on the cattle though. The ground is a mixture of sand and gravel with the occasional hard rock. Be prepared to see many lame cattle at the end of the trip but hopefully we won't suffer too badly."

The suffering of the animals made Johanna's heart

clench. She knew her pa and the other men needed the cattle for their fresh start in Oregon. They had no choice. There was no other way of getting the cattle there. But it was still horrible to watch the number of abandoned, lame or dead animals as they made their way along the trail. The stench was disgusting and made worse by the flies. The grass was very thin making it even more difficult on their cattle.

She couldn't do anything about the cattle but she could help the oxen. When they stopped for the evening, she gathered some cornmeal and a little molasses. Mixing it together she gave a little to each of the oxen.

"What are you doing, girl?"

Johanna jumped. She hadn't seen her pa coming. "They need it, Pa, they worked so hard today pulling the wagon over those horrible rocks."

Something in her tone must have pulled at her pa's heart strings as he didn't lecture her about wasting food. He simply patted her back. "You got a soft heart just like your mother."

She was saved from replying as Captain Jones blew his bugle summoning the men to his side. Johanna prayed it wasn't bad news.

* * *

"WHAT DID CAPTAIN JONES WANT, PA?" Becky asked as the family sat down for their evening meal.

"He reckons there is going to be a storm tonight. Says we need to tie everything down."

Becky and Johanna exchanged glances. Becky wasn't scared of anything but even she didn't like lightning. Johanna was terrified of it.

"Pa, can I watch the lightning? Can I? Please, Pa."

"No, lad, I want you safe. Lightning's nothing to be messed with." Pa stroked Stephen's hair as if to tell him it wasn't a rebuke.

"Johanna, isn't that Carrie Ellis crying? She seems to be calling for you."

"I best go see what's wrong. Maybe Mr. Hughes is on guard duty."

"He'd have told you rather than leave the girls alone. Wouldn't he?"

"Usually, yes, he would but somethings wrong."

Johanna hurried over to the wagon.

"What's wrong, Carrie? Why are you crying?"

"I hate lightning. It scares me. Sarah is scared too." Carrie's shoulders heaved as she sobbed. "Uncle Rick said he wouldn't be long but he's been gone ages."

"He had to go find some cattle," Sarah clarified. "Do you think he will get caught in the lightning?"

Johanna hoped not. "There might not be any tonight.

So let's not worry about that now. What story would you like?"

"A magic one." Carrie piped up before Sarah could answer.

"Come here to me, both of you." Johanna cuddled the girls as she told them a bedtime story about magical witches and far away kingdoms. "Now go to sleep and dream about your prince charming."

She kissed both girls—Carrie was already asleep and Sarah's eyes were closing.

"Thank you, Jo, you always make us feel better."

Johanna smiled at her, in a way feeling envious of the young girl. She wished she still believed in faraway castles and princes. She stayed by their fire until Rick returned. He came back, look tired and more than a bit frazzled. She handed him a plate of food and some coffee.

"How did you know I didn't eat?"

"I guessed from what the girls said," Johanna stood up. "I have to be getting back."

"Can't you stay a little while?"

She was tempted. She hesitated just a few seconds too long.

"Please sit, have some coffee."

She didn't want to as she was still angry over his decision about the girls, but he looked so miserable she didn't have the heart to say no.

"You look too tired to talk, so please let's not talk about the girls," she said as she poured some coffee for both of them.

"I don't want to fight, I just want to talk."

She nodded. Maybe by spending time with him she could influence his decision. Ma always said it was better to give a man an idea and then let him think he thought of it in the first place.

"Thank you for the book. I am enjoying it immensely," she said stirring her coffee for something to concentrate on. Her eyes kept being drawn to his face and she didn't want to give away her feelings.

"Have you cried yet?" His gentle tone suggested he knew the answer.

"You mean after reading about the plight of all the orphans?" As soon as she asked, she wished she could take back her words. The look on his face almost made her reach out to hug him. Instead, she quickly stood up. "I have to go. Sorry."

She didn't wait for his response but walked quickly back to her family.

* * *

THERE WAS no lightning and for that Johanna was thankful. But the winds rocking the wagon from side to side were fierce. She watched the canvas move back and forth as the wind howled. The cattle bellowed. Poor animals were scared too. She didn't get a wink of sleep so she rubbed her blearily eyes when it was time to get up.

A scene of devastation greeted her as she got down from the wagon. Tents were upside down, some of the young boys were trying to catch canvases flying off in the wind. She saw her pa talking to another man all the while shaking his head.

"What's wrong with Pa?"

"Nothing, but his friend lost a few of his cattle," Ma answered. "He didn't round them up properly last night. Captain Jones told us to keep them inside the wagon circle but he ignored him. Now your pa is going to have to go help round them up."

"What can I do to help you, Ma?"

"You don't look like you got much sleep either. Why don't you and Becky take turns and try to have a nap today? I don't want either of you getting sick."

"Yes, Ma." Johanna had no intention of napping but she couldn't wait to get back to her book. Oliver had just met Fagin. She was enjoying it immensely. Half of her wanted to ration out the pages so it lasted more of the trip. The other half wanted to read it in one sitting.

It didn't take long to find the wandering cattle and the wagons started off again. They traveled until they met the Big Sandy River where they finally found decent grass.

* * *

"WE WILL BE CROSSING the Green River in a couple of days."

On hearing her pa's voice on the other side of the wagon, Johanna held the pan so tightly her knuckles turned white. She had heard stories about this river. It was seen by many to be more dangerous than the Platte. That crossing, in which Millie's husband had been injured had been bad enough.

"Don't tell the girls about it yet. We don't want to frighten them," Ma whispered back obviously not realizing Johanna stood within earshot.

"We've been lucky on the river crossings to date. Jones knows what he is doing."

"He does but even he can't control nature. We've seen enough graves to know how many die by drowning."

Johanna gulped at the sound of tears in her ma's voice.

"Della, don't take on so. You're stronger than that."

"I am sick of being strong, Paddy Thompson. I am fed up of this trip. I never want to see another wagon until the end of my days, eat another meal cooked in the open or see a buffalo chip. I have had enough."

"Aw, Della, don't be like that. We have fared better than most. Our daughter has got herself a fine husband, we haven't lost any family members and have held on to most of our belongings."

A rustling sound suggested her pa had embraced Ma. "Look at that view. Have you ever seen mountains that beautiful? They are majestic. Just you wait, we will be over them and in Oregon before you know it."

"We have at least three months traveling still ahead of us, Paddy."

"Yes, we do, me darling, but just imagine how good our lives will be at the end of it. We shall be surrounded by our daughters, their husbands and our grandchildren. The farms will do very well and we will all be comfortable. You believe me, Della, don't you, darling."

"I know I would follow you to the end of the earth and back again. But grandchildren? I hope you are praying the wedding takes place first."

Pa roared laughing then silence reigned.

Smiling, Johanna set the pan down and retreated away from the wagon. She knew her parents loved each other, and although she was a little guilty at listening to their private exchange, it made her feel good knowing the harsh trip hadn't diminished their affection for one another.

CHAPTER 12

*J*ohanna stared at the mountains around them. She was driving, her pa instructing her. Captain Jones had insisted everyone learn to drive the wagons just in case they were needed. Johanna knew it was his way of preparing for more calamities ahead. They had been traveling steadily downhill for the last number of hours, their snow-capped surroundings a reminder of what was to come. The weather, although thankfully clear of rain, was a little cold. She wished she had changed from her cotton dress into a woolen one.

A hideous scream rang out echoing via the mountains. Pa grabbed the reins, his strength helping to stop the wagon.

"What was that?" Johanna asked, her voice wobbling as the screams continued. "Indians?"

"Stay here." Her father's curt response made Johanna pause. But she only waited long enough for him to move away from the wagon before following him. Someone was in trouble and she may be able to help.

There was a crowd of men around one of the wagons. She couldn't see anything but the injured man was moaning loudly.

"Miss Thompson, maybe you should go back to your wagon."

Johanna hadn't noticed Rick until he spoke.

"I am not a child, Mr. Hughes, I may be able to help."

Johanna pushed past the crowd of onlookers. There was a lot of blood but her eyes were focused on the victim. Joey Freeman. He was still alive. She rushed to his side where his sister was trying to help.

"Sheila, what can I do?"

"Nothing but pray. It's all any of us can do."

Johanna pulled the girl into her arms as Sheila broke down sobbing. Looking over her shoulder, she caught sight of her ma coming holding a bottle in her hand. She watched as Mrs. Freeman gave Joey some laudanum. Quite a lot of it. She caught her ma's gaze but her ma gave a slight shake of her head.

"What happened?" Johanna asked, more to distract Sheila than out of curiosity.

"Joey fell and the wagon rolled over him. Pa couldn't stop it in time."

At Johanna's intake of breath, Sheila shuddered. "Why Joey? He hasn't done anything to anyone. If he's dying, why let him suffer? Why couldn't he have been killed straight away?"

"I don't know, love. Do you want to come for a walk?" Even as she asked, Johanna knew nothing would have kept her from Stephen's side if, God forbid, something similar had happened to her brother. But Sheila was different. She had been sickly at school and her parents had cosseted their only daughter to the point she could barely make a decision for herself. But Ma always said it was at times of great trial that people's real character showed through. Sheila gave Johanna one tight hug, wiped her eyes and then walked steadily over to Mrs. Freeman and Gracie who had just arrived on the scene.

* * *

SHEILA DREW the older woman into her arms comforting her just as Johanna had done for Sheila a few minutes before. Johanna couldn't bear to stay near the family.

Joey's labored breathing and cries of pain were enough to drive anyone mad. The fact that he was only a year or so older than herself didn't help. What if it had been Rick lying there?

She knew she was being selfish thinking of Rick at a time of such sorrow but what if he died on this trip without them ever getting the chance to be together. She was tempted to go to him and tell him of her solution to his problems. She would marry him. But that was too forward. Anyway, it was total madness to even be thinking like this when a school friend lay dying. What was happening to her? She climbed into her pa's wagon and started praying for a quick relapse for Joey.

It took almost two hours for Joey to die. It seemed like nobody in the whole wagon train moved during that time. She couldn't remember it ever being so quiet, well apart from Joey's groans and Gracie's sobs.

"Johanna, come out here and help me prepare some food for the Freeman's and Mr. Bradley. There is no way Gracie or Mrs. Freeman will be cooking tonight."

"Yes, Ma."

"It's a horrible business losing a child. Not right. It's against the laws of nature for a parent to bury their own child."

"Ma, what will Gracie do now? She was practically

engaged to Joey. Everyone knew they would end up married when we got to Oregon."

"Gracie's young. She'll find someone else eventually but, in the meantime, she will need a good friend. Sheila too."

Johanna nodded. She couldn't imagine how she would feel if Rick were to die. She only knew him a few weeks. Gracie had grown up with Joey. She set about her chores hoping by keeping busy it would make her too tired to think.

* * *

JOEY WAS BURIED LATER that evening. Captain Jones said the prayers in the absence of a man of the cloth. Johanna rubbed a wet cloth over her face and tidied her hair before taking her place at the graveside. She watched with sadness how Sheila supported her ma while her pa stared dumbstruck into the grave of his son. Gracie's reaction worried her the most. She wasn't sobbing anymore but looked stricken staring at the ground.

Johanna caught Rick's eye above the crowd and they exchanged a sad smile. She now had an inkling of how much pain Rick had been in, losing his sister and nephews. Johanna hadn't ever lost someone close to her before. She had good memories of Joey making her and her sisters laugh. She was determined that was how she would remember him.

It was time for the train to start moving again. Someone had spotted Indian tracks and they were keen to put some distance between the wagons and any tribes on the warpath. Captain Jones insisted the wagons roll over the burial site so by the time the last wagon rolled out, there was no sign of Joey's resting place.

"I used to think he was very disrespectful when he first told us to drive over the graves," Becky said to Johanna as they gave one last look back at where their friend now lay. "But it's to stop the Indians from digging up the body and taking the clothes."

Johanna shuddered.

CHAPTER 13

*C*aptain Jones led them to a beautiful spot beside the river. The water flowed clear and fast and tasted wonderful. There was plenty of grass for the cattle and oxen to graze. He suggested spending a full day here. The men would use the time to grease the axles and make sure the iron tires were fitting properly. The wagons had to be in the best possible condition for the trip over the mountains.

Early the next morning, most of the men had headed out to hunt so the families could stock up on their provisions. Dried meat being better than nothing. Ma and a few of the other women had taken some laundry down to the river where the children were enjoying a swim. There were only a few women and children remaining in the camp, catching up on chores and rest.

"Johanna, come here. Now," Becky squeaked.

Johanna came out of the wagon where she had been trying to find some thread to mend the rip in her skirt. She stared at Becky who was looking white faced into the distance. She followed her sister's gaze to discover about twenty Indians had ridden into camp. She faltered as she tried to climb out of the wagon, her limbs were shaking so much.

"What do they want?" Becky whispered out of the side of her mouth.

"I don't know, Becky, but there is no war paint." Johanna hoped it meant they were just visiting.

"Go find Ma and the others and tell them to stay by the stream," Becky said walking slowly toward their visitors.

Johanna wasn't about to let her sister go alone. She spotted Julia standing looking at the Indians, a star struck expression on her face.

"Julia, run down and tell your ma and mine to stay by the stream. You stay with them until we come and get you." Johanna hoped her school teacher's tone would make Julia do what she said without asking questions. It didn't work. Julia kept staring at the Indians. "What are you going to do, Johanna?"

"Julia, move now." Johanna gave her a hefty push in the direction of the stream. She made sure the little girl was running in the correct direction before she followed Becky.

The Indians dismounted as they approached. By a use of broken English and sign language they asked about their train and where the men were.

"Nearby," Johanna lied. "Gone to the stream to fish for supper." She mimicked the actions of fishing causing more than one Indian to laugh. Some of the Indians broke away and started to look curiously inside the wagons. They didn't seem to be looking for anything in particular. Then a brave spotted a corset on a bush where the owner had left it to dry. He tried it on his head making his friends laugh loudly. Johanna had to hide a smile as its owner, Mrs. Newland, who hadn't endeared herself to anyone because of her constant complaining turned bright red.

"Jo, what do you think they want?"

"I don't know, Becky, but if they were going to do anything, they would have done it by now. It's obvious the men aren't here."

The Indians seemed in no hurry to leave. They tasted the food the women had been cooking by dipping their fingers into the pots. If it pleased them, they shoveled the food into their mouths with their hands. If they didn't like the taste they turned the pot over in disgust.

When they did this to Mrs. Newland's cooking, she hit one Indian with her ladle.

Johanna and the other woman held their breath as the angry looking Indian held his wounded hand up to his mouth taking a threatening step toward Mrs. Newland. A couple of words from their leader were enough to make him walk away.

"He is sorry, he make mess. Not right to waste food," the leader said. "Indian squaw be mad too."

"Becky, what if we get some biscuits or cookies? Maybe then they will leave." Becky nodded before she moved toward their wagon to see what Ma had available. Johanna went to follow but what she saw unfolding made her blood run cold. She had read about Indians taking young girls to become slaves and then wives. She hadn't noticed Carrie sitting by her uncle's wagon. Now an Indian was standing over her, examining her as a horse trader examined his animals. Instinctively, Johanna moved toward them. She watched the leader as he rubbed young Carrie's face. He seemed to be trying to get her freckles off. Johanna moved closer not wanting to upset the Indian but also determined to get between him and Carrie. The poor child was struck dumb with terror, her eyes wide blue pools in her pale face. Maybe the Indian was just curious. He seemed to be looking at Carrie's freckles.

"Not paint. On skin." She pushed Carrie behind her and showed the brave some freckles on her arms. He rubbed her arm and grunted when the freckle stayed the same. He spat onto his hand. She took her arm back quickly in case he meant to use his spit to wash her clean. That was a mistake as it made him look her in the face.

He said something in his own language before he reached up to her hair and pulled her braid loose. Her heartbeat raced as he slowly pulled the pins from her hair making it flow around her shoulders. His actions attracted the attention of some of the other braves. They moved closer. And closer. Johanna's heart raced. She felt Carrie loosen her grip on her skirt. The child moved quietly. Johanna stared at the brave but he didn't seem to notice the young girl slip away.

CHAPTER 14

ohanna held her breath as the Indian's scent filled her nostrils. He obviously didn't bathe regularly but it was more than that. He smelled like an old bear rug someone back in Virgil had made. She hoped her stomach contents wouldn't make a reappearance. She couldn't help taking a step back as he came closer. Then he yanked a knife from his pocket. Johanna froze while a couple of women screamed. He moved closer holding the knife. She wanted to back away but her feet couldn't move.

Instead, she stared at his eyes. He didn't look angry or fearsome but curious. She didn't know what he wanted but instinctively knew he wasn't going to hurt her. The blade made a singing noise as it glided close to her scalp. He stood back grinning, his hands holding a long tress of her hair. "For my squaw."

Then he whistled and all the Indians made a run for their horses, mounted and rode off. They were gone as quickly as they had come. Johanna hadn't moved. She stood in the center of their camp frozen to the spot.

* * *

THE CAMP TURNED into uproar with women and children crying. Becky kept asking her if she was all right but she couldn't speak. She wasn't capable of anything but simply stood where the Indian had left her. Her limbs started shaking, she saw people coming toward her but she couldn't say a word.

The smell of mint filled her nostrils as he came up behind her and placed a rug gently around her shoulders.

"Come on, let's get you back to your wagon," Rick spoke softly. "Can you walk or will I carry you?"

"I can walk, if you give me your arm." She took hold of his arm as her legs felt like jelly. She wanted her ma.

"Is Ma back?"

"She's at the wagon. Your sister thought it best for her to wait there."

Johanna didn't answer. She guessed Becky was

giving her a couple of minutes to compose herself before she frightened their ma. "Ma will be upset he cut..." She shuddered thinking of the sun glinting off the blade.

"Don't think about it. He didn't mean to hurt you. They aren't used to seeing such golden hair. He probably wondered whether it was as silky as it looks."

Johanna wondered if they were still talking about the Indian. She glanced up at him to find him staring back at her.

"Carrie told me you saved her life."

At that Johanna laughed. "Your niece has a flair for dramatics. I did no such thing. He didn't want to hurt her, he just wanted to see why her freckles, which he thought was paint, wouldn't rub off."

"You didn't know that, not for certain. So thank you on her behalf."

They reached the wagon. With a sob, her ma launched herself at her. "My baby, are you hurt? Becky told me how brave you were."

"I will leave you to it, good evening, Miss Thompson, Mrs. Thompson."

And he was gone. Her ma fussed around her but Johanna couldn't help wishing he had stayed.

$\mathcal{E}$veryone was keen to leave the campsite despite the pretty location. The visit from the Indians, although pretty harmless, had spooked them all. A couple of the men had boasted how they would have shot the braves dead if they'd been there when the visit took place. Johanna was very glad the women had been left alone as otherwise a massacre could have taken place. They had no way of knowing how many Indians populated the mountains but it was easy to see they knew their way around better than the white emigrants.

The cattle were well grazed and they'd had a chance to fill their water containers and get some laundry done. As they pulled out of the campsite, Johanna couldn't help wondering what the Indian squaw had thought of her present. If Rick came home to her with another woman's hair as a gift, she would throw him out of the house and make him sleep in the barn. She colored despite the fact nobody else could read her thoughts. Good thing too. She barely knew Rick Hughes.

They crossed a couple of streams as they made their way forward. The ground was rough going due to the number of rocks in their path. Most people got out of the wagons to walk rather than be jolted like milk in the churn.

"They call this place the Devil's Backbone. Captain Jones has scouted ahead looking for the best route down."

"It's pretty though, Pa, isn't it?" Johanna commented as they looked around their surroundings. "It looks like an artist painted the snow on top of those hills."

"They aren't hills, Johanna, that's the mountain. They may look pretty but I am not looking forward to crossing them. You can see from here how sparse the vegetation is. Our cattle will struggle."

Johanna guessed her pa was right, but she didn't want to fill her mind with gloomy thoughts. She waited with the rest of the wagons until they got the signal to move forward.

"We only made ten miles today but the animals are tired. I don't like the look of those clouds so let's get the shelters up as soon as possible." Captain Jones' orders were passed down the trail from one driver to the next. Johanna looked at the sky hoping they wouldn't be in for more thunder and lightning. She had just got down from the wagon when the first hailstone hit her.

"Ouch, that hurt."

"Quick, girl, get under the canvas with your ma."

"But what about our chores, Pa?"

"They can wait. Do as I say."

Johanna watched from the canvas opening of the wagon as the women huddled in the wagons and the men in tents taking shelter from the hailstones. They were bigger and rounder than any she had seen back in Virgil.

"Why don't you bed down here, girls. Looks like that storm won't pass now till morning."

"Aw, Ma, I'm hungry."

"You are always hungry, Stephen. There are cold biscuits by your head. Eat one of them."

Johanna was too tired to eat so took her ma's advice and settled down to sleep. She thought it would be impossible given the noise of the stones on the canvas but she underestimated how tired she was. When she woke again the storm was over, the sun rising on a beautiful but slightly colder day.

CHAPTER 16

The next few days proved difficult. The continuous light rain made traveling more uncomfortable. Pa was worried about his animals—the grass was sparse and of poor quality. "The oxen won't be much use to us in the mountains if they lose too much weight now."

"Don't fret, Pa. There will be better grazing. Captain Jones said so," Becky commented as she stirred something on the fire.

Pa didn't reply. He had fallen asleep on the fold up chair he sometimes used.

"Your pa and the rest of us are exhausted. I think Captain Jones should make camp at the next suitable spot and let us all catch up on your chores and our sleep."

"I'm sure Captain Jones knows what he is doing, Ma, he has done this before."

"You watch your tongue, young lady. You are not too big to feel the back of my hand."

Becky rolled her eyes at Johanna but made sure her ma didn't catch her. Later when their parents were asleep the girls lay under the tent, listening to the soft rain against the canvas.

"Jo, do you ever wonder what it will be like in Oregon?"

"Sure, don't you?"

"Sometimes. But often I just wonder, will we ever see it?"

Johanna sat up. Becky, while impulsive and often foolhardy, was usually the positive person in the family. It was unlike her to be so glum.

"Are you feeling all right, Becky?"

"Doesn't it get to you? Every day we pass them."

"Pass what?"

"The graves. Some days I count upwards of eight or nine."

Johanna put her arm around her twin. "Of course it upsets me, but I try not to think about it. We have been very lucky so far. We haven't lost many people."

"We've lost enough. Mrs. Ellis and her children. I know they weren't with us from the start but they still died. Mr. Long and Joey were really nice people. Why did they have to be the ones who died?"

"Becky, you got to stop thinking like this. We don't know why some die and others don't but we have to keep going. We have to believe we will end up in Oregon. I will be a teacher and you will be a farmer's wife. Although I still can't get used to you wanting that. Back in Virgil, you wanted nothing more than to be the banker's wife and have a large clothing budget. Have you really changed so much?"

"Scott wants to settle down on his own land. I heard him tell David. He isn't going to plant crops but he wants to raise horses. Seems he has some already."

"I didn't think wagon masters got paid a lot of money. I would have thought horse ranches were expensive to start." Johanna had heard that was true. Their pa couldn't afford to have a horse ranch and he'd been relatively well off back in Virgil. Maybe it was different in Oregon.

"I don't know. I couldn't hear everything. But he did say he wanted to settle down. I want to be with him. I don't care if it's in the middle of town or out in the middle of nowhere. So long as he is there. With me."

"You really do care for him, don't you?"

"I love him. Just as much as Eva loves David. I just wish he saw me as a woman and not a child. When he does notice me, it's to yell at me for being childish. He seems to think I am going to break down in tears or fall apart at the slightest thing. I am not Sheila Freeman." Becky's hand went to her mouth. "I shouldn't have said that. Sheila is so different now from when we were at school. Back then she would get the vapors if one of the boys brought a spider to school. Now look at her. I saw her driving the wagon the other day."

Johanna had seen it too. Her ma had explained Mr. Freeman was ill and Mrs. Freeman wasn't willing or able to try to manage the team. So Sheila had stepped up to the job. The girl had certainly changed.

"Can't you see Captain Jones is concerned for your welfare. Why else would he check up on you all the time?"

"He delights in pointing out my errors. He kept telling me off yesterday for the way I was directing the team. I might not be as strong as Pa, but I am a capable driver. I drive better than you and he doesn't say anything to you. Ever."

Johanna smiled.

"I don't see what is so funny. My heart is breaking and you are laughing."

"I am not laughing. You are being silly. Why would any man constantly check up on a woman if he weren't interested? Captain Jones doesn't talk about me because he doesn't notice me."

"He thought you were very brave over the Indians. You were. I was so proud of you."

"You were brave as well. You tackled them first. I just happened to get nearer the one who wanted our colored hair."

"Do you really believe he likes me, Jo? You wouldn't just say that, would you?"

"Becky, I do think he likes you but…"

"But what?"

"Nothing. It's late and we need our sleep."

"I can't go to sleep now. I want to know what you were going to say."

"I just wondered if you would be more successful with Captain Jones if you stopped fighting him all the time." Johanna took a deep breath waiting for Becky to say something but she didn't. "You go out of your way to be difficult around him."

"I do not," Becky protested but she didn't sound convinced.

"Yes, you do. You present a very disagreeable picture. Always arguing and wanting your own way.

"That's because he is insufferable when he thinks he is always right. He is only human."

Johanna giggled earning her a dirty look. It only made her laugh more and soon Becky was laughing too.

"All right. I admit, I might be slightly quarrelsome towards him."

"That's an understatement."

"Yes, dear sister, thank you for pointing out my obvious lack. I shall try better in future. What do you suggest I do?"

"Be yourself, Becky. Never try to be anyone else. You are perfect the way you are and if Captain Jones can't see that he isn't the man for you."

"You are very wise at times."

"You got the beauty and I got the brains." Johanna lay back down. "Actually, Granny told Eva you would never settle for someone like Ben the banker. She said you needed a strong man to keep you in line."

"She makes me sound like a mulish ox."

"Well…" Johanna giggled again.

Becky smiled back at her as she lay down. Then she put her head on her elbow studying her sister.

"What? Do I have stew on my nose?"

"I can't see in the dark. I was just going to tell you, you are wrong you know."

"Well, that's a change. I thought you were going to make an effort."

"No, I mean it, Jo. I didn't get the beauty. You are beautiful inside and out. I love you."

Johanna was so startled by her sister's declaration she was struck dumb. She knew Becky cared for her, of course she did but her twin was never one for voicing her feelings.

"I love you too, Becky. Night." She included Becky and Captain Jones in her thoughts that night hoping the two of them would find their way to each other. Becky's soft snores filled the tent leaving Johanna alone with her thoughts. Why she saw fit to give her sister advice when she was so bad at handling her own love life was beyond her. She had never minded before, being the quiet twin. Becky had always been the one in the limelight, the one people noticed. But when Rick was around, Johanna felt beautiful and as if she was the only woman in the world.

CHAPTER 17

"Thank goodness that rain has stopped, it's almost impossible to get a fire going and cook some decent food."

"Ma, you are a miracle worker. I don't think we have passed one day where you couldn't cook something."

Ma beamed at the praise even though she pretended to ignore it.

"There are some toll bridges up ahead. Captain Jones said it will cost one dollar per wagon to cross the two bridges."

"Does Mrs. Long have the money to pay?" Ma asked Eva who had finally given in and was sharing their fire and provisions.

"David told me to pay it on her behalf. At this point,

we are like one big family. If any of us go anywhere, we all go together."

Ma nodded. "I wonder what Mrs. Long will do when she gets to Oregon."

"She's spoken about claiming some land next to ours but David is trying to convince her to set up a small boarding house in a nearby town. He thinks it would be easier on her than trying to raise the girls and run a farm."

"I guess it would, although your pa says there are so many single men out in Oregon, she may marry again."

Eva shuddered.

"What? Don't tell me the thought didn't cross your mind?"

"It didn't, Ma. I don't think Pa would get married again if anything happened to you. I know I wouldn't look at another man if David were to…" Eva swallowed hard. "I am not even going to finish that thought. Let's think about something more cheerful."

Johanna saw her ma give Eva's arm a squeeze. She shivered, their conversation bringing back thoughts of Joey. He and Gracie had their whole life planned out and now she was left alone. She wondered what Gracie would do when they got to their destination. It wasn't a question she was about to ask.

* * *

"JOHANNA, look there's another wagon train. Can we go over and say hello?" Julia asked practically jumping up and down with excitement. "There may be some children we can play with."

"We can say hello but don't go wandering off, please, Julia." Johanna found it hard to deny the young child anything. She had been so resilient after the loss of the father she adored. She took her time approaching the wagons. They didn't want to be mistaken for Indians.

"Hello there, young lady. You sure have brightened up my day."

She didn't like the look in the stranger's eyes or his tone. Maybe coming over to the train was a mistake.

"We are traveling just behind you. Julia wanted to say hello and see if there were children traveling with you."

"All these kids ain't yours, are they? You look mighty young."

"No, of course not." Johanna regretted snapping as his eyes grew narrower. "Come on, children, let's be getting back. Your parents will be worried."

"Tell your folks we are camping here for the rest of today and tonight. We will have some card games later if your men want to lose their wallets."

His uncouth laughter followed her back down the

trail. She shivered despite the warmth of the sun. Thankfully, there was nobody as bad as him traveling in their wagon train. Well, apart from Harold and his friends but they were gone now.

"I didn't like that man, Jo," Almanzo said. "He had mean eyes."

"Well, we don't know him. Maybe he just wasn't in the mood for visitors." Johanna almost choked sticking up for the stranger, but she had to practice what she preached. You shouldn't judge anyone until you got to know them. She had no intention of getting to know that particular man any better.

* * *

THEY REACHED CAMP. Mindful of what had happened when they met the Indian some weeks previously, Johanna sent Almanzo to tell Captain Jones about the wagon train. She wasn't surprised when he sought her out later.

"Afternoon, Miss Thompson. Almanzo tells me you came across a wagon train camped up ahead. Must be the one whose tracks we saw yesterday. Did you speak with them? Have they been experiencing any problems?"

"I did speak to one man but not for long. He

mentioned the men were welcome to visit tonight to play cards. I didn't ask him anything about the trail."

Johanna didn't meet Captain Jones eyes. It was normal to ask any traveler they met about conditions on the trail. Previous travelers often left signs telling those that were coming behind them to watch out for bad water or alkali grass. She should have at least inquired whether the train had been hit by any illnesses. Measles and other diseases were contagious.

"He had mean eyes and was looking at Jo in a funny way," Almanzo added making Johanna's face flush scarlet.

"Almanzo, go on now. Captain Jones has things to do. Why don't you go tell your pa about the wagons?"

The boy scampered off.

"What was the man like?" Captain Jones asked.

"He seemed pleasant enough."

"What Johanna means is he gave her the creeps," Becky said. "My sister is too nice to tell you herself."

"I think Captain Jones should form his own opinion," Johanna snapped back at her sister before addressing Captain Jones. "I know you will want to speak with their leader."

"Yes, I will, thank you, Miss Thompson." He tipped his hat at Johanna and walked away leaving Becky fuming.

"Did you see that? He just ignored me. Well, I never."

"Becky, darling, you will never catch a man with a spiteful tongue. I thought you were listening the other night when I suggested you stop being so quarrelsome."

"I only said what you were thinking."

Johanna didn't bother to argue. There was no point in trying to explain to her twin that some things were better left unsaid.

* * *

PA CAME BACK LATER that evening to tell them they had, in fact, found two different wagon trains.

"Talk about opposites. In the one Johanna met, they are playing cards and drinking whiskey. In the other they are reading bibles and singing psalms. I was tempted to visit the first and then have my sins removed by a visit to the second."

"Paddy Thompson. How could you?"

"I was only joking, Della, don't take on so."

"That is not my idea of a joke and certainly unfit for your children's ears."

Johanna saw her pa throw his eyes up toward heaven but it was her ma's reaction that concerned her. Her ma was rarely in bad temper and she usually would not correct their pa in front of them.

"Ma, why don't you go lie down for a while? Becky and I will finish up here."

Becky nodded, exchanging a look of concern with Johanna. Pa had already walked off obviously put out by his wife's rebuke.

"Where is Stephen?"

"He's playing with Julia Long. Are you feeling all right, Ma? You seem flushed."

"I think it's too much sun. I will be fine after a lie down. Thank you, girls."

The twins watched as their ma made her way to the wagon. Instead of making up a bed underneath like she usually did, she climbed into the back. Her actions were as slow as a lady double her years.

"I don't like it, Becky. I think Ma is coming down with something."

"She's as fit as a fiddle, Jo. You heard her, she will be fine tomorrow."

CHAPTER 18

*J*ohanna checked her ma after they had cleared up. As she feared, her ma was running a temperature and was obviously unwell. She climbed out of the wagon.

"Becky, go get Eva please."

"What's wrong? Is it Ma?" The fear in Becky's eyes reflected her own.

"Hurry."

Becky lifted her skirt and ran in the direction of Eva's wagon. It was a good job their ma was laying in bed ill as if she saw the amount of ankle her daughter was flashing she would have a heart attack.

Johanna went to the fire, putting on a kettle to boil some water. She had no idea whether it worked or not but some of the older folk had said sick people found cooled boiled water easier to tolerate. The doctor back in Virgil had told them to add salt to the water if they ever got sick. Johanna did so even though she wasn't sure what illness she was treating. It wasn't long before Eva came back.

"What's wrong with Ma?"

"I don't know, Eva, but I think it might be cholera."

The sisters looked at each other. Cholera anywhere was a death sentence but out here in the wilds, there was little hope.

"Where is she?" Eva made to move toward the wagon but Johanna stopped her.

"No, don't go near her. You could get sick too. I will nurse Ma but can you take Stephen? Becky should go to stay with you too."

"Over my dead body, "Becky exclaimed hotly before realizing what she had said. "I am not leaving you alone to nurse Ma. I will help."

"So will I," Eva said firmly.

"No, Eva. You need to stay healthy for David and Pa. Stephen needs to be looked after." Johanna looked at the resolute expression on Becky's face. "Becky and I will nurse Ma. You tell Pa to stay clear. You should also tell Captain Jones."

"I am sure he will wait to break camp until Ma is

better," Becky added before turning to add more fuel to the fire.

"Don't be too sure of that, Becky. You heard him back in Virgil. He is not going to wait for sick people." Eva responded.

"But that was then. Before he got to know us. He wouldn't leave me...us behind."

"Let's not worry about that now. We need to concentrate on Ma." Johanna's firm tone got her sisters' attention. "We are going to need more sheets and cloths. We have to keep Ma drinking and sponge her down to get rid of the fever." She looked toward Eva who was looking at their ma's wagon, heartbreak written all over her face. Johanna put a hand on her older sister's arm. "Ma is strong, Eva."

"But I should be here."

"Your place is with your husband. Ma will fret over Stephen if he stays here."

Eva walked away, her shoulders slumped. Sometime later, Pa arrived in a state.

"Where's Della? I need to see her."

"Ma said you have to stay away Pa, she doesn't want you getting sick."

"To heck with that. She's my wife."

"Yes, she is and she won't get any sleep if you keep roaring out here. Do what your wife says Mr.

Thompson and stay away. The less people in contact with Mrs. Thompson the better." Captain Jones spoke firmly.

Pa stared at him for a couple of seconds but must have realized he was right as he turned to go. "Can I not do something to help?"

His voice, so unlike the confident tone her pa usually used, made Johanna want to cry but there was no time for that.

"Pa, we need water and fuel for the fire. Some meat broth might be good too."

"So she can still eat?"

At the hope in her pa's eyes, Johanna could have kicked herself.

"Not yet, Pa, but when she can, she will need to build up her strength."

With a last lingering look at his wagon, her pa slowly walked away.

CHAPTER 19

"Be honest with me, Miss Thompson. How ill is your mother?" Captain Jones asked.

"Very ill. I don't know if it is cholera or mountain fever. She has several symptoms." Johanna looked anywhere but at his face. She didn't feel comfortable discussing her mother's bodily habits with anyone, let alone a man.

"I will get you extra water and fuel. Is there anything else you need?"

"No thank you."

"Is your sister helping you nurse her?" His tone was different and he wouldn't look her in the face.

"Becky insisted. I tried to talk her out of it but you know what she is like."

"I am starting to find out. I appreciate the steps you

have taken to keep everyone else safe. I will check back with you later." He moved away just as Becky stepped out of the wagon.

"Captain Jones, a minute, please."

He stopped. Turning slowly, he ran his hand through his hair. Johanna caught the troubled look in his eyes.

"I assume you have told the entire train we are camping here until Ma gets better." The silence that greeted Becky's words spoke volumes. "You can't mean to leave us here. You wouldn't do that."

"I don't want to do it, Miss Thompson, and believe me, if I could think of any other way I wouldn't. But as I explained that day in Virgil, the safety of the entire wagon train is my concern."

"But a couple of days won't hurt." Becky's hurt made her tone more strident.

"They might. You've seen for yourself the weather has got colder even though we are still in July." Captain Jones fiddled with his hat so much, the material was in danger of ripping. "I can give you a day. After that, we will have to move on."

Afraid Becky would burst into tears, Johanna stepped forward.

"Thank you, Captain Jones. We are sure Ma will be better tomorrow."

He looked into Johanna's eyes, and she saw how tormented his decision had been.

"Captain Jones, we do understand. Becky, come on, we need to give Ma another bath."

Rolling her sleeves up further, Johanna busied herself getting a bucket of water ready. She couldn't face the fear of being left behind now. She would deal with that tomorrow. Her ma needed every ounce of energy now.

Pa came back later with fuel and water but he didn't linger. Eva brought some food for her sisters and some extra bedding.

"I do wish you would let me help."

"Go, please, Eva. If one of us gets sick, we will need you to help then."

"Eva, David needs to speak to Captain Jones. He's told us he will only camp here till tomorrow then he is leaving with or without us."

"I know, Becky."

Johanna caught the acceptance in her sister's tone but Becky missed it.

"David is going to be able to talk him into staying, isn't he?"

"No, Becky, he isn't. Captain Jones called a meeting a while ago. A couple of wagons have sick people too. He can't make any exceptions. Mr. Price and many of the other men wanted to leave right away. We were lucky to get until tomorrow."

Johanna put her arm around Becky for her own comfort as much as hers. "Becky, we don't know what tomorrow will bring. Let's just concentrate on Ma."

Becky nodded before taking the bucket of water back into the wagon. Saying goodbye to Eva, Johanna put some water on to boil. She had to wash out the sheets.

CHAPTER 20

Early the next morning, Ma wasn't any better. Becky had insisted Johanna get some rest, so she'd fallen asleep in the tent leaving her sister with their mother. She heard someone moving about outside and then smelled bacon frying. She got up quickly expecting to find her pa at their fireside. Instead, it was Rick Hughes.

"Oh, it's you. You shouldn't be here."

"That's a fine welcome this early in the morning."

"I'm sorry, but Ma is very ill. You should have been warned."

"I was." He didn't look up from the bacon.

"Yet still you came?" Johanna thought she must be dreaming.

"I guessed even a burnt breakfast would be better than nothing. My cooking skills have only improved slightly, but I got you more water and some more fuel."

"Thank you for helping us but you should go."

"I am not leaving you, Miss Thompson. I am staying put. If Captain Jones must carry on, we will catch up later."

"But the girls?"

"The girls will be fine. They will stay well clear of your wagon."

Johanna didn't know what to say. She stood staring at him wondering at the emotions in his eyes. Pity, understanding, and something softer.

"I won't abandon you." He stared at her so intensely she had to look down. She wouldn't be able to keep her emotions in check if she continued looking at him.

"You really mean it? About staying?"

"Yes, ma'am. You and your family were kindness itself to my family when we had problems. I won't leave you alone out here. I may not be a good nurse or cook, but I can chop wood and fetch water. I can also fire a gun."

"Thank you." It seemed such a little thing to say after his rather grand gesture.

He nodded to the fire. "Now you are up, you might

want to take over. It's looking rather singed around the edges."

They exchanged a smile that had Johanna's heart racing. Her fingers shook as she moved the bacon around the pan. He was gone when she turned around to say thank you again.

CHAPTER 21

"*J*ohanna, where are you?"

Eva obviously couldn't see her. She was catching up on some laundry while their ma slept. She left the sheet in the tub and walked back toward the wagon and her sister. "Over here, why? What's happened?" Johanna saw the look on her sister's face. "Who?"

"Pa, Mrs. Long, and Julia's sisters, Rachel and Louisa. Sheila Freeman is feeling ill. Gracie too."

"What about Stephen?"

"He seems fine."

"And David?"

Eva didn't answer, her eyes filled with tears. Johanna gave her a quick hug. "He's young and healthy, Eva. He will be fine," Johanna said and looked around her. "We need more water and more fuel. We should bring the sick people all together so we can nurse them properly. Also keep the young ones, Julia, Stephen and any others as far away as possible."

"Is it true? Pa's sick and David?" Becky came running back from the direction of the stream. "Julia said lots of people are sick."

"Yes, but we cannot panic. Becky, can you ask Julia and Stephen to collect more fuel? It will help them to feel useful," Johanna asked as she took Eva's arm. "Come on, we will have to move the sick."

"I will move the sick. You get the tents ready. I think there may be a storm coming."

Never was she so glad to see someone. Rick's calm voice helped to steady her.

"Are you feeling all right?" Her concern for him made her voice shake a little.

"I am fine. Are you getting enough rest?" He pushed a tendril of hair back from her face and for one insane moment she wanted to turn into his shoulder and weep. But that wouldn't help anyone.

She nodded, not able to speak.

"The girls seem well too, although Sarah was quiet this morning and wouldn't eat anything. I am not sure she is sick though."

Sarah was still grieving for her mother and brothers.

Still, it was worth keeping an eye on her. "Maybe you should go back and check on her before moving the others."

He nodded, the concern on his face making her hope she was wrong.

* * *

SHE HEARD A NOISE, possibly thunder. Looking up at the sky, she saw the black clouds in the distance. As if they didn't have enough to deal with. Rain would make everyone more miserable. Johanna pushed the hair back from her face. She wasn't going to worry about the weather now. She had more important things to do—like search everyone's wagon for their supplies of Camphor. She was running dangerously low.

"Johanna, I can help. Please let me."

"Go back to bed, Ma, you are too ill. If you get worse, Pa would never forgive me."

Rick came back helping those who could walk, making several trips to carry those he couldn't.

"Sarah is sick too," Rick said, putting out his hand to Johanna. "I've asked Stephen and Julia to keep Carrie with them. Mrs. Newland will look out for them."

Johanna's resolve faltered when she saw just how sick Sarah was. She was so thin already and now the vomiting was taking away any chance of giving her nutrients to survive. "You can't die on me. I won't let you," she repeated over and over to the young girl.

Eva, Mrs. Freeman and Johanna took turns to mind those who were ill, resting when they could. Some of the other women minded the children and cooked for everyone. The men who were well, had to combine guard duty with finding food. There had been reports of Indians on the warpath. For now, it was a fight between two tribes, but nobody fancied getting caught in the middle.

CHAPTER 22

*L*ater that day, Captain Jones arrived to check on the patients. Johanna wasn't feeling very well but she had sent Becky to rest.

"Miss Thompson, you look...strained."

"Thank you, Captain Jones." She smiled to show him she was joking, although she felt as bad as she probably looked.

"How are your mother and father?"

"Ma is getting better, Pa isn't any worse and Becky has just fallen asleep. Are you here to tell me you are leaving?"

"The wagon train will leave in the morning."

She had known what was coming, but it was still upsetting to hear him confirm her thoughts. But as he stood there, she wondered if she had missed something.

"Yes, Captain Jones?"

"There was a meeting earlier. Your family have made a real impact on this train and several of the wagon owners have refused to leave without you."

"But you said they were going tomorrow. My parents won't be ready to leave by then. They will get much worse if they have to travel by wagon."

"That won't be necessary, we will stay as long as we can. Another two days or so."

"We?"

"Mr. Price has agreed to lead the other wagons. Seems he doesn't rate my abilities very highly."

"I don't think he rates anyone very highly, Captain Jones, but I will miss Almanzo."

"And he you, Miss Thompson. He was very upset at the thought of leaving you behind."

"Who else is staying?"

"The Bradleys, the Newlands, Rick Hughes, Milly and her husband as well as the families of those who are ill."

"The Newlands?"

"Yes, I was surprised too. Mrs. Newland put her foot down and refused to leave while people needed help."

Johanna wanted to pinch herself, but not just for misjudging Mrs. Newland whom she had thought to be a whiner. She couldn't believe all these people were going to stay with them. Her eyes watered but she didn't want to break down in front of Captain Jones.

"How are the other sick people?"

"A couple of them are getting better."

"But some died?"

"Yes, ma'am, some died. I think that is some of the reasons so many folk want to leave with Mr. Price. He seems to think you can catch whatever it is through the air."

"He may well be right. I don't know how Ma fell sick or even if she has the same thing as the others. I am not even sure what illness they have. It may be mountain fever. I think cholera would have been deadly."

"Usually, but some have recovered from it too. Your mother is a strong woman, and she has good nursing. Both count for a lot."

Too embarrassed to say anything, Johanna stayed quiet.

"But you and your sister are not ill only tired?"

She hid a smile at the concern in his voice knowing she was not the real reason for his worry.

"We are both fine but thank you for asking. A couple of days' rest and we will all be back to normal."

"Good, as the journey ahead of us will have some more challenges."

Johanna couldn't think of a suitable reply so stayed

silent. She watched as he stared at the tent Becky was sleeping in for a couple of seconds before tipping his hat and walking away. She couldn't help wondering if his decision to stay had been because of Mr. Price questioning his ability or if it was something more than that.

Now wasn't the time for speculation. There was plenty of work to be done before she had to give her patients their next bath.

CHAPTER 23

*J*ohanna was about to take a rest when she saw a man coming out of her tent. "Stop, what are you doing? Becky? Is that you?"

Becky turned around wearing a pair of trousers and a shirt. "I borrowed them from the Freemans. They were Joey's."

"But why are you dressed like a man?"

"We need more food. Captain Jones won't let me stand guard duty so I am going to get us our dinner."

"You can't go out there alone, Becky. Anything could happen."

"I could die here. Who knows how many of them are going to make it?" Becky glanced in the direction of the ill people. "Pa didn't know my name this morning. He is real bad. Sheila Freeman thinks Joey is still alive. I have to do something, Johanna. I can't just wait around for them to die. We all need something more substantial to eat. Pa said he fancied rabbit stew."

Johanna half smiled at the reminder of her father's favorite dish. It wasn't the time to remind Becky their pa could barely keep water down.

"Go on then but for goodness sake be careful."

"I always am!"

* * *

"Miss Thompson, have you seen your sister?"

Johanna stilled. She didn't want to answer Captain Jones but couldn't ignore him. "Eva is over there looking after her husband."

"Not Mrs. Clarke. Rebecca?"

"Not since earlier. Don't worry about Becky, she can look after herself."

"She may think that but I don't believe it and neither do you. If you did, you wouldn't keep scanning the horizon. Do you want to tell me where she went?"

His tone said she didn't have a choice. Anyway, he was right, she was concerned and, despite the fact he would be angry, he would go looking for Becky and bring her back.

"She has gone hunting for food." At the expression

on his face, Johanna balked. "She's an excellent shot, nearly as good as Pa."

"Your Pa would have more sense than to go out alone when the Indians are at war. Does your sister ever engage her brain?"

There was no appropriate response to that comment.

"Jo..." The weak voice interrupted her exchange with Captain Jones.

"Captain Jones, don't be so hard on Becky. She had to do something. Everyone is so ill. She thought some fresh meat would help them. Given your men are tied up with chores and guard duty, she thought it would help."

"Typical of her not to think of her own safety," he muttered as he strode off.

Sending a look of apology in his direction, she went to Sarah's side.

"Yes, darling."

"Jo, will you look after Carrie. Promise me."

"I will look after her until you get better and then you can take over." Johanna's tone was meant to be reassuring but her voice sounded far too shaky.

"I want you to promise. Carrie loves you."

"We all love you, Sarah. You have to get better. Carrie needs you. So does Rick."

A look of disbelief came over Sarah's face before she closed her eyes. For a second, Johanna thought she had gone, but she had just passed out. She stayed by her side trying to get her fever to come down. It was sky high. She didn't know how long she stayed by the child's side but she was there when Rick returned.

"How is she?"

"I can't get her temperature down. I think she's given up."

"She can't do that. I won't let her." Rick reached over Johanna and picked up Sarah. He carried her toward the stream.

"What are you doing?"

"Something I saw back East, although it was a bath of cold water not a river. We have to try. I am not losing another one of my family."

Johanna didn't try and stop him. She wasn't sure anything would save Sarah but at least Rick would know he tried everything. She wanted to stay with him but she had to get back to the others. Her pa, Gracie, and Sheila Freeman were critically ill. The others were still sick but seemed to be recovering.

CHAPTER 24

*R*ick bathed Sarah again and again in the freezing river water. At first, she had whimpered against the cold but now she wasn't reacting at all. He prayed as he washed her. How had he ever believed he could leave this child in an orphanage? He loved her as much as he could love his own child.

"Come on, Sarah, fight. We need you. Carrie and I need you."

There was no reaction.

"Carrie will be all alone if you die. You have to get better. You have to."

He spent ages with her, brushing the hair back from her face. "Come on, darling. I love you. You have to show me how to look after your sister. Please."

After a while, her eyelids fluttered and she looked up at him.

"I love you."

She closed her eyes again but he thought she seemed stronger. He carried her back to the camp where Johanna was waiting.

"Is she any better?"

"I think she might be. She spoke to me."

Johanna's look made his heart turn over. She ran her hand over his arm.

"Let me change her and put her back in bed. I have some boiled salted water for her to drink."

"Thank you, Jo. What can I do to help?"

"Eva could do with some assistance. David wants to have a bath and I don't think it's appropriate for me to do it." Her cheeks turned a pretty pink. He leaned over and kissed her forehead quickly.

"I will see to it. Talk to you later."

Johanna busied herself seeing to Sarah. The change in the girl was nothing short of a miracle. Not only had her fever abated, but she seemed to be fighting back too.

"Welcome back, little lady, I missed you," Johanna whispered to the young girl. Both Sarah and Carrie had taken a special place in her heart. It wasn't just because she spent so much time with them but both girls had been so brave following the loss of their ma and brothers. She wanted to protect them from ever being hurt again. Something that was impossible to arrange, especially given their current situation.

"Jo?"

"Yes, darling."

"I didn't go to Heaven, did I? I thought I went to be with Ma." A tear ran down the little girl's face.

"No, honey, you stayed here with us. Your uncle Rick wouldn't let you leave him. He loves you so much."

"Really?" Hope blazed out of Sarah's eyes.

"Yes, darling, really." Johanna hugged her close. "Now you get some rest. When you wake up, I will give you some soup."

The expression of distaste on Sarah's face clearly showed how she felt about the soup but she didn't argue. She closed her eyes and was soon snoring softly. Johanna sat with her for a while pushing the hair back from her eyes.

* * *

RICK HELPED Eva to bathe David.

"He is much better already, isn't he?" he said to Eva as they walked David back to the camp.

"Yes, thanks to Johanna. She's a wonderful nurse. I don't know where she learned all she did," Eva replied.

"From her books, she said. Although I think some of her knowledge comes from her natural consideration for others."

Eva gave him a look but she didn't push him to answer the question it contained.

"I hope you will listen to your wife and take things slowly for a few days, Mr. Clarke," Rick said in a bid to change the focus of the conversation.

"David, please. Every time anyone calls me mister, I look for my father." David smiled. "As for your question, I believe you know that it is better for one's health to listen to the Thompson sisters when they give orders."

"Hey, that's enough of that. Anyone would think I was bossy," Eva exclaimed but the twinkle in her eyes showed relief her husband was on the mend.

Eva INSISTED David rest again after they returned to camp. As soon as she was finished helping Johanna, she returned to find him napping in their wagon. She lay down beside him as quietly as possible but his eyes opened.

"You need to sleep and get your strength back."

"Come here and give me a kiss. That will help more than any amount of sleep."

Eva kissed him before losing control of her emotions. She sobbed as he held her close.

"I am so sorry but the last few days have been horrible. I was sure I was going to lose you," Eva said, sniffing back more tears.

"Darling, I didn't wait for you all those years so I could leave you now. We are going to have a wonderful life in Oregon. Just you see."

"I hope you are right." Eva looked at him, her eyes checking his skin for signs of illness, his eyes for fever.

"Eva, I am better. Stop fretting or you will make yourself ill. Thanks to you and your sisters, I am almost back to full strength."

"Johanna has been amazing, hasn't she? And to think Granny thought she would be the one least suitable to traveling the trail. I hate to think what would have happened to Ma, Pa, and you if she had stayed in Virgil."

"All the Thompson women are incredible. But I have a firm favorite. Now are you going to talk all day?"

Eva saw the glint in his eyes. Smiling widely, she kissed him gently. "Are you sure you are well enough?"

"I will let you be the judge of that," he whispered as he nuzzled the side of her neck. All thoughts of conversation fled.

CHAPTER 25

Becky stood admiring the view. The mountains were all around her, to her back and sides. They looked like magnificent cakes capped with white icing. She didn't feel menaced by their size. She believed one hundred percent in Captain Jones' ability to get them over their slopes and on into Oregon.

She took a couple of steps relishing the freedom of wearing pants rather than her calico dress. If only Ma would let her dress like this all the time. It made doing chores so much easier. She had been lucky in her shots this morning having killed a couple of small animals. Hopefully, the sick patients back at camp would appreciate the addition of fresh meat to their diet.

"I could shoot you myself."

Becky whirled around to find herself looking at

Captain Jones. He was furious. She took a step back from him.

"I didn't hear you."

"Obviously. I could have been anyone. What would you have done if I had been a tribe of Indians?"

Flustered, Becky didn't know what to say. She walked a little away from him trying to think of an answer.

"Well, you aren't so it's pointless discussing that," she said hoping her tone didn't show how his nearness was affecting her.

He took two strides and she was in his arms.

"I don't know whether to kiss you or kill you." He gathered her to him in the fiercest of kisses. His mouth found hers but not in a gentle caress. He pulled her closer still as she wound her hands around his neck, giving herself up to his embrace. All too soon, he pushed her away from him.

"Miss Thompson, I apologize. That was unforgivable."

"Why? You like me and I like you. What's wrong with that?"

"Everything. I am a grown man while you are still a…"

"Don't you dare call me a child. Not after kissing me like that. I am a woman and I know my own mind." She picked up the animal carcasses before she stormed off, her temper carrying her across to her horse.

* * *

HE WATCHED HER GO, her body shape clearly outlined in the pants and shirt she was wearing. She was beautiful, not just physically. Her independence and willingness to fling aside society conventions only made her more attractive. She didn't seem to be afraid of anything. He thought he had seen everything when she broke David out of his jail but this was yet another side to her. How many young ladies would set out into the unknown to hunt for much needed food for sick people? None.

But much as he admired her and found her attractive, he shouldn't have kissed her. For all her bravado, she was an innocent. She deserved to be courted by a man from her own kind. Not an orphan who'd been brought up by a combination of mountain men and Indians. What would she say if she knew he had been married before? Maybe she wouldn't care but her pa would. He was not the type of man any decent father wanted as a husband for their daughter.

* * *

BECKY KNEW he was following her, but she refused to wait for him. He had almost called her a child. After the way he had kissed her, she had finally thought he saw her as the woman she was. But no, he still insisted she was a child. She had behaved like one, letting her temper get the better of her by walking out on him but if she had stayed, she may have hit him. He intrigued her, and not just because he hadn't fallen at her feet like all the other men she'd known. Becky wasn't big headed but she knew she was very attractive to the opposite sex. She'd had a string of admirers back in Virgil. No doubt Scott Jones would call them children as well. But it wasn't just the boys she had seen giving her the look. Their fathers were also not immune to her charms. In fact, Scott Jones was the first man who hadn't given her the usual look and if she was honest, that is what had attracted her to him at first. He was a challenge, one she was determined to crack. But that initial attraction had soon subsided. Her feelings for him had become very real. She admired his strength and his honesty. He stood up for what he believed in and wasn't afraid to show it. She knew he was brave. You didn't cross the country a number of times without having courage. But it was more than that. He had stuck by David regardless of the so-called evidence against him. He had seen Harold for the spiteful, nasty individual he was from the start. If

CHAPTER 26

$\mathcal{T}$he days and nights seemed to merge into each other as she and Becky nursed the sick and the dying. They used the same treatments for everyone. They administered camphor until their supplies ran out. Johanna insisted everyone, whether they were ill or not, drank cooled boiled water. All the patients received sponge baths using mint tea to bring down their temperature. It worked for some but not for everyone. They lost an older lady who had been traveling with her son and daughter-in-law. They also lost a baby and a young boy.

Johanna had been worried about Milly and refused to let her help. She insisted her pregnant friend was more useful minding Stephen, Julia and the other young ones. Julia's sisters were recovering as was their ma, but they didn't have the energy to keep up with the young'uns.

Pa and Sheila Freeman seemed to be recovering, although the same couldn't be said of Gracie.

"She isn't getting any better, is she?" Becky asked Johanna.

"No. It's as if she's decided not to fight. I can't think of what else to do."

"Gracie, it's Becky. You got to get better, darling. Your poor father is beside himself at the thought of losing you."

Johanna wiped away a tear as she listened to Becky trying to convince Gracie to fight back. She knew her twin felt a little guilty. She had been jealous of Gracie's interest in Captain Jones even though it hadn't lasted long. Gracie's soulmate had been Joey Freeman. Maybe she wanted to be with him.

"I think we should ask Rick to carry her down to the stream. It worked for Sarah. Her fever broke."

"But isn't it dangerous?"

"It can't be any riskier than leaving her here."

Becky went to find Mr. Bradley to ask his permission. Once she had gone, Gracie's eyes fluttered open.

"Johanna."

"Yes, Gracie." Johanna moved quickly to her side.

"Will you look after my pa?" Gracie's voice was so weak, Johanna had to lean closer to her to hear her. "He will be all alone now. He should get married. Maybe Mrs. Long."

"Shush, Gracie, you need to rest easy and conserve your energy."

"I want to be with Joey. Please don't stop me."

Johanna wiped the tears away furiously. "I can't just watch you die, Gracie."

"Please, Jo. I don't have a life without Joey. I…" Gracie's voice trailed off giving Jo a shock, but her friend had just fallen asleep.

Mr. Bradley gave his permission reluctantly. He wanted to be the one to help Johanna but she insisted he needed to rest. He wasn't as ill as his daughter but he was older too. Rick carried Gracie to the river but it was Johanna who bathed her, Rick turning his back for the sake of propriety. Gracie didn't fight back even when Johanna accidentally let her face slip under the water. Crying softly for her friend, Johanna and Eva dried her before wrapping her in a clean dress. Then Rick carried her back to the camp.

They repeated the process with Sheila Freeman. Sheila wasn't as weak as Gracie and was able to help

Johanna a little. Rick carried her back to camp as she was too weak to walk herself. Sheila joked about it being a rather drastic way to get a man's attention. Everyone laughed. Rick squeezed Johanna's hand quickly. She glanced up to catch him looking at her softly. She smiled back at him before moving to check on her next patient.

* * *

JOHANNA WAS GIVING Sheila another bath with the mint tea. Johanna hummed as she rubbed Sheila down.

"I like that song," Sheila mumbled.

"Do you want a drink?"

Sheila nodded. Johanna held her up while she drank.

"How is Gracie?"

Johanna looked away. She didn't want to upset Sheila but she wasn't about to lie either.

"Tell me."

"She says she wants to be with Joey. She won't even try to fight the illness."

"Poor Gracie. And Joey." Tears ran out of the corners of Sheila's eyes.

"Sheila don't cry, please. You'll set me off."

"You are so strong, Johanna, caring for all of us like this. Thank you."

Sheila fell back asleep. Johanna eased back on her

ankles about to stand up when she felt a strong arm at her side.

"You need a break."

Rick more or less marched Johanna away from the sick tents to a clearing near the river. There he had laid out a blanket with some food and some water.

"You can't do anyone any good if you get sick. You need to eat something and you need to rest."

"But what about…"

"Taken care of. Mrs. Freeman, Eva and your ma have it in hand."

"But Ma is weak."

"Your ma has recovered and is worried about you. Let her help. You will ease her mind. And mine."

Johanna smiled at him gratefully. She wasn't hungry but her whole body yearned for sleep.

"I know you are tired and you can sleep in a minute but first eat this. It will keep your strength up. You cannot fall ill just as everyone else in getting better.

"Not everyone. Gracie isn't."

"Gracie doesn't want to. You can't change that."

"But I can't just let her die."

"You are not God, Jo. You have to let Him do what he decides is best. You have done your utmost to help everyone. Now you have to have the strength to accept what comes next."

"Do you really believe that?"

"Yes, I do."

"But what about Sarah? She had given up too."

"Sarah is a child. Gracie is a young woman. It's different. Sarah has her whole life to live for. Gracie believes hers is over."

"But she may meet someone else."

"She might but she could spend the rest of her life missing Joey. Either way it's not our decision to make. Is there anything you could have done differently for Gracie?"

Johanna shook her head.

"Then that's what you must remember. No matter what happens, you did your best and that is all you could do. Now eat and then sleep."

"But..."

"You know I sympathize with your father," he interrupted her gently. "You are a very stubborn woman."

She was about to argue when he kissed her fiercely. "Eat. I can't bear the thought of losing you. Not now. Not ever."

He held her closely for a moment as if trying to pour his strength into her.

"Eat, please. Just a little. For us."

"Well, when you put it like that, how can I refuse?"

She said the words playfully, but her eyes mirrored the love in his.

"I believe I love you, Miss Thompson."

"I love you too, Mr. Hughes."

This time she kissed him.

CHAPTER 27

The next twenty-four hours passed very slowly. Becky went out hunting again but this time David Clarke went with her. Captain Jones had insisted and David was feeling well enough to ride. To Johanna's amazement, Becky hadn't argued with Captain Jones' decision. They didn't stay out long but brought back some small animals for the pot. Mrs. Newland was in charge of the cooking, so Becky came to see if she could help Johanna.

"What is happening here? How are they?"

"Pa has turned the corner and is improving. Ma is with him. Sheila Freeman's ma is with her. She is much better as is Sarah." Johanna took a deep breath before adding, "There is no change in Gracie."

"That's good though, isn't it? I mean if Gracie had really given up, she would be dead by now."

"Rick, I mean Mr. Hughes, helped me give Sheila and Gracie a bath in the river. The cold water definitely helped bring down their fevers."

"Thank God nobody else died, I couldn't bear to have to stand at another graveside. I have had enough of death to last me forever."

"You and me both," Johanna agreed vehemently.

* * *

AFTER BATHING Sarah and checking on Gracie, Johanna sat down. For once the chores could wait. She needed a rest. Her thoughts turned to her granny. The old woman had always said, "If you practice a gratitude ritual, your worries would always be smaller." Johanna realized she had a lot to be grateful for. Instead of falling sick in one of the barren areas of the trail, their current location was ideal. There was plenty of good water, the meadows were full of grass for their cattle to graze on and the scenery, once you took notice of it, was inspiring. She sat looking at the mountains wondering what it would feel like to be on top of one looking down at the valley.

* * *

She must have fallen asleep as she found herself tucked up in bed sometime later with no memory of how she got there. She was still wearing her clothes, only her shoes were missing. Becky was nowhere to be seen but she heard laughter coming from the wagon. She started to walk toward it when the world started spinning. She would have fallen over if Eva hadn't reached her in time.

"What are you doing up? You should be in bed."

"But what about Ma and Pa and the others?"

"Everyone is doing great. Thanks to you and Becky. Becky has gone for a bath and Ma is visiting with Pa."

"Did Gracie die?" Johanna dreaded asking the question but she had to know. To her relief, Eva smiled.

"No, she didn't. She is still sick but with some good luck, she will be fine. Seems Sheila had words with her, something about throwing her life away when Joey didn't have that choice."

"That was a little harsh, wasn't it? She was very ill."

"Harsh or not, it worked. She's alive." Eva's tone suggested she agreed with Sheila's actions.

Johanna could hardly believe it. She was sure Gracie would die. "How long have I been asleep?"

"About sixteen hours. Mr. Hughes dropped off some fuel for the fire and found you slumped over near the wagon wheel. He picked you up and put you in the tent before coming to fetch me."

"He put me to bed?"

"He did but all he took off was your shoes so your dignity is still intact." Eva's teasing would have made her smile, but her thoughts were consumed by Rick.

"Back to bed with you. I am going to heat up some stew, and I want you to eat up every bit. You've lost weight in the last few days. You cannot afford to lose any more."

"Yes, Ma!"

Eva laughed at the joke as she headed over to the fire to stir the pot of stew cooking there. Johanna realized she was ravenous. She couldn't remember the last time she had eaten. She continued sitting not having the energy to walk back to her tent.

"You look peaky," Pa's greeting woke Johanna. She had fallen asleep in the sunshine.

"So do you. Are you sure you should be out of bed so soon?" she asked, concerned about the paleness of his face.

"I am feeling wonderful now, daughter. You and your sister have done us proud. We are all alive because of you girls. Thank you." He leaned down and kissed the top of her head before disappearing. Johanna rubbed the spot he had kissed. Her father was not an affectionate man. It simply wasn't done to hug your children. She knew he loved them but these rare shows of affection affected her deeply.

"My cooking isn't that bad you know. You didn't have to fall asleep to avoid eating." Eva teased her once more but she could see by the expression in her sister's eyes, she was worried about her. Johanna made an effort to sit straighter to pretend she felt better.

"I'm sorry, Eva. I will eat later. For now, I just want to have a bath and sleep."

"I'm coming with you. I wouldn't put it past you to fall asleep in the stream."

They met Becky on her way back, her eyes gleaming. Somehow Johanna didn't think it had anything to do with her dip in the stream.

"I take it the water is nice?"

"Life is wonderful isn't it."

Eva and Johanna exchanged a look before bursting into giggles like two school children. Becky sailed past as if she hadn't heard them.

"I think someone is in love," Eva commented as they walked toward the stream.

"I think it may be two sided. Why else would Captain Jones stay with us?"

"Well, to be fair, I guess he didn't have much of a choice. Mr. Price accused him of all sorts of things including being responsible for Harold and his antics. Said it was his fault the wagon train had fallen behind schedule. I was shocked by how many agreed with him. Seems people have short memories."

"That they do. I am sorry the wagon train split, but I am glad Mr. Price is on the other one. I did not like that man."

"Not many did."

CHAPTER 28

*L*ater that evening, Captain Jones called them all together.

"I think we can all agree we have had a lucky escape thanks in part to some fine nursing by the ladies of our camp. Everyone has pitched in and worked together and for that I am grateful."

There was a round of applause.

"I have decided to stay in this spot for the next forty-eight hours. Our head nurse, Miss Thompson, has advised me that even though our patients have nearly all recovered, they still need rest. Fresh supplies of clean water are also vital for their survival."

The crowd murmured but nobody spoke up.

"Does everyone agree with my decision?"

"Captain Jones, both Rebecca and Johanna played a

part in saving my girl and Joey's girl. We will do whatever they want us to do." Mrs. Freeman's voice quivered as she spoke.

A lot of people in the crowd nodded.

"You are the boss and we will do as we are told. No whining," Mrs. Newland added causing many to laugh out loud. Johanna watched as the smile lit up Mrs. Newland's face too. There was no doubt the stress of the last few days had brought that lady's true character to the forefront. She had told Johanna she and her husband hoped to find some family members who had gone ahead of them. They hadn't been heard of since they left Independence, but neither had she seen their names on any graves. Mrs. Newland had only one child, the others having died in infancy. "I know I whined too much earlier on the trail. I was so certain the next grave we would pass would belong to our son or his family. I know now I was wrong. I should have had more faith."

"We all react to our fears in different ways. You have been wonderful over the last few days. We couldn't have managed without you."

"Thank you for the kind words, child, but I think we both know you are the reason our people lived."

Johanna blushed at the praise. She didn't like being the center of attention.

"What will you do when you get to Oregon?"

"I would like to become a teacher."

"That's a fine choice for a woman like you. You have such a natural way with children. It will keep you busy until your own family come along."

Johanna smiled back reminding herself Mrs. Newland was a similar age to her ma and, therefore, would hold old fashioned views. Still it rankled that everyone expected her to give up teaching once she became a wife. Why couldn't she combine both roles? Men did. But she didn't have the energy to discuss that now.

CHAPTER 29

"Pa, some of the cattle are sick. What should I do?"

Her pa was still weak after his illness so Becky had taken on the job of looking after their cattle.

"Mix some molasses and vinegar and give it to them. It will help counteract the effect of alkali on their system. Dumb animals should know not to eat that grass."

Becky thought her father was expecting too much of the animals but she wasn't about to argue. He wasn't used to being ill and was in terrible form. He had scolded her for dressing like a man but when he realized how many of his chores she had taken on, he had stopped. Her ma didn't say a word, something more concerning than if she had yelled at her. Ma being so quiet meant she still wasn't feeling herself.

"The roads seem a little rough, Becky?"

"Yes, Pa, there are some mud holes. I've been trying to avoid them but it's difficult."

"You are doing your best, lass, and that's all that matters."

Becky glowed, her father rarely gave compliments.

* * *

THEY REDUCED their pace over the mountains. "Miss Thompson, you need to slow down a little. The passages up ahead are likely to be treacherous. This continuous light rain isn't helping any."

Becky couldn't stop herself wondering if he was telling the men the same thing. But she didn't question him. She had to stick by her decision to show him she was mature. Only a child would argue with the leader of their train. He waited for a few seconds and she had to restrain herself from smiling at the confusion in his eyes. Clearly, he had expected her to argue. Well, she was going to keep him on his toes by behaving differently to what he expected. He raised his eyebrows as if he could read her thoughts but still she didn't change her expression. With a sigh, he moved on.

Soon it became obvious he was right as she struggled to maintain control of the wagon. Not that she would admit it to him. She wished her pa and David were feeling better. Her arms ached from trying to control the oxen who must have smelled water ahead as they surged forward. Finally, Captain Jones called on them to make camp. There was good grass for the animals but the mosquitoes were out in force. Becky had been bitten so often, she didn't think she had a piece of her body not showing the scars of these horrible flies.

"Miss Thompson, you did very well controlling your wagon tonight."

Becky glowed from the unexpected praise. "Thank you," she said.

He waited as if he expected her to say something else. She scratched her arm, a particularly nasty mosquito bite was driving her nuts.

"If you take a buffalo chip into your tent or wagon and set it alight, it will keep the mosquitos away. Won't smell too pleasant but I guess right now, you won't care."

She smiled her thanks but again didn't say anything. She was determined to act the part of a young lady even if she was wearing pants.

"Well, goodnight then, Miss Thompson."

"Goodnight, Captain Jones."

She didn't smile at the perplexed expression on his

face until he had walked away. Then she allowed herself to laugh. Maybe playing at being a lady was going to be more fun than she'd thought.

"It's nice to see you smiling, dear, although I do wish you would give Joey's clothes back to Mrs. Freeman."

"She told me to keep them, Ma. They make doing the chores so much easier. I don't have to worry about catching my skirts in the fire or getting them caught on the wagon axles."

"Well, don't get too used to them. Soon we will be in Oregon, and I expect my daughter to return to being a well brought up young lady."

Becky sighed. The idea of being a lady had once more lost its appeal. She couldn't bear the thoughts of corsets and petticoats just now. She hated feeling so constricted, especially in the heat. Men certainly had the better deal.

CHAPTER 30

*J*ohanna had snuck out of the wagon to take a walk. She had seen Rick walking toward the river and hoped to make it look like she had bumped into him. She hadn't seen him alone for days and was really missing him.

As soon as he saw her, he took her in his arms, kissing her soundly. Waves of heat tingled through her body. She slid her arms around his shoulders. His hands trailed down her back settling at her waist, pulling her closer to his body. She clung to him as he kissed her tenderly at first before the kiss deepened. When he suddenly pushed her behind him, she squeaked in protest.

"There's someone coming," he whispered.

Johanna squinted but she couldn't see anything.

"Who is it?" There was no response to Rick's question. "You best head back to your wagon," he whispered to Johanna, pushing her in the right direction.

"It's Captain Jones," she whispered back before moving toward the captain.

"Evening, Captain Jones, is everything all right?"

"No, it isn't. Thank goodness I found you, Miss Thompson, it's a boy. He's very ill. Bring some water."

Johanna ran to the wagon, grabbed a canteen and made her way back carefully to where Captain Jones was crouched beside a small body.

"It's Almanzo Price. Look at the state of him." She gave him some water but the majority of it trickled back out of his mouth. He was burning up with fever.

"Can you carry him over to our fire before you go searching for his family? They must be around here somewhere."

"I will carry him to Miss Thompson's wagon." Rick bent down to pick up the small child.

"But why would he leave their campsite?" Johanna asked helplessly.

"Maybe they are sick, too, and he came for help? Goodness knows he shouldn't be out here alone. Not at his age and not this sick," Captain Jones said. "I will come back to check him shortly."

Johanna put some water on to boil before stripping the child of his vermin-laden clothes. They were no better than rags. What had happened to the Price family for Almanzo to end up in this state?

"Rick, you best go back to the girls. They will be upset if more people arrive in this state."

"Will you be all right?" He touched her cheek tenderly.

"Go, please. I have to concentrate on Almanzo."

He left and she turned to contemplate the boy in front of her. She examined his body as she sponged him down with mint tea. The brew seemed to cool his skin. He had some marks on his body as if he had been beaten. Johanna pursed her lips. Mr. Price had not been known for his gentle ways but even still, those bruises went too far.

She would have words with Almanzo's pa when they caught up with him.

"What on earth?"

Eva put a hand to her mouth at the sight of the poor young boy.

"He's burning up with a fever. Captain Jones found him on the edge of the campsite. We think he may have come for help?"

"Where is his family? The rest of the wagon train?"

Johanna shrugged her shoulders. Almanzo wasn't in

CHAPTER 31

Captain Jones reappeared the next morning. His face was grim.

"Did you find his family? Are they dead?" Johanna asked hoping against hope he had some good news.

"I found some fresh graves and some wagon tracks. I recognized some of the names as members of our train..." He stopped talking leaving the silence linger a little too long.

"They must have been hit by the sickness too. Was Mr. and Mrs. Price there too?" she prompted, developing goosebumps on her arms despite it not being cold.

Captain Jones was staring at her but it didn't seem like he saw her.

"Scott? What is it? What's wrong?"

Johanna took a step back as Becky moved closer to Captain Jones, putting her hand on his elbow. The touch seemed to reach him. He blinked rapidly before speaking. "I found the graves and some wagon tracks."

"Yes, and..." Johanna couldn't help feeling she was missing something. Of course the wagon train would have moved out, but then why was Almanzo on his own?

"I think Almanzo was left behind."

"What? Why? Who would do something like that to their own child?" Johanna threw the questions at him but he was looking at Becky. She watched her sister reach up to his face and push his hair out of his eyes before she stroked his cheek. Embarrassed at witnessing such an intimate moment, Johanna pulled back. She turned her attention to nursing her patient. She felt rather than saw the couple walk away.

* * *

SOMETIME LATER, Becky reappeared. "How is the boy?"

"He hasn't woken yet. I think his fever may have broken but you know what it's like. As soon as we think we have won, the fever returns more aggressively than before."

"Johanna, can we walk for a bit?"

Johanna was about to decline but her sister said, "Please."

She moved a bit away from Almanzo but was reluctant to go too far.

"I don't want him to hear what I have to say," Becky explained.

"He's unconscious."

"Yes, but he could still hear us. What I have to say isn't for his ears."

"What? Has this something to do with Captain Jones? Where is he by the way? I saw him and some of the other men ride out earlier."

"They went back to the other campsite."

"But why? I thought everyone had left."

"He said he saw the tracks of wagons. What he didn't tell you was some of the people who were left behind hadn't been buried."

Johanna's stomach heaved.

"You mean they left their dead unburied. Who would do such a thing?"

There was no answer. Becky just stared at her.

"What?"

"I think it might be worse than that."

"What could be worse?"

"Scott, I mean Captain Jones has reason to believe

some of those left behind weren't dead. At least not when the wagons left."

"You mean... No. Nobody would do that. He must have got it wrong."

"He didn't."

"Oh, Becky, how could they? Those poor people."

"They were going to do it to Ma. Remember?"

"That was different, they were going to leave us with her. Not alone to fend by herself. Is that what he thinks happened to Almanzo's family? Are there any of them left alive?"

Becky shook her head.

"Oh my God. What will I tell him when he wakes up? A ten-year-old boy left alone in the world. How cruel."

"He might not be alone. Oh, Jo, Scott didn't find Almanzo's parents. They weren't with the others."

"Maybe they'd been buried?"

"There were names on all the graves."

Johanna couldn't speak. The thoughts going through her mind were too horrible to put into words. Wordlessly, she turned back.

"What will you tell him?" Becky asked softly.

"Nothing." She looked back at her sister. "I will wait to see what he can tell me. Captain Jones must be mistaken."

The look in Becky's eyes showed Johanna her sister didn't agree but she didn't say anything.

"Jo, don't wear yourself out. You are already tried from nursing Ma and the others. Let us help."

Johanna nodded, too weary and sad to answer. She made her way back to Almanzo. Thankfully his fever wasn't any higher, and he was still asleep. She stayed with him for the rest of the night, refusing Becky and her ma's offers of help. "He knows me best. I want to be by his side when he wakes up."

"Jo, he is very ill. We don't know how long he was left alone. He may not recover."

"He will, Ma. He has to."

Captain Jones came by early the next morning to check on the patient but also to tell Johanna they had to pull out. "I'm sorry as I know it's not what you want to hear but we lost so much time already."

"Yes, of course. We can mind him in our wagon. Stephen can stay with Eva."

"I'm sorry about...well, the things I shared with Becky. I gather she told you."

"Yes, she did but until Almanzo can speak, I think it's best not to jump to conclusions." She saw the pain in his eyes the minute she spoke. She was sorry as it hadn't been her intention to hurt the captain but the reality of a child being abandoned by his own parents was just too awful for her to contemplate. At least not without proof.

"Good day, Miss Thompson." His tone was as cold as the ice in his eyes.

"Captain Jones, please don't misunderstand me. I am very grateful for everything you did for those people. I just prefer to hear what happened from Almanzo."

He tipped his hat and strode away.

CHAPTER 32

They travelled for hours that day at a strong pace. They were climbing the steep hills and the traveling was taxing on everyone but particularly the animals whose hooves were cut on stones and other obstacles on the road. Someone suggested making rawhide booties for the oxen so the women started sewing these.

"I don't know how the Indian women can make clothes out of these skins. I can barely get the needle through it," Eva complained.

"Sewing was never your strong point, sister dear," Johanna couldn't resist teasing Eva even when her sister stuck her tongue out at her in reply.

"Captain Jones is intent on having us catch up on the

time we missed. I just hope he is not pushing himself too hard. He barely took a rest when everyone was sick."

Johanna knew Becky was concerned and while part of her understood, she was more worried about the boy in the back of their wagon. He still hadn't regained consciousness. When they made camp, everyone was busy with their chores. Eva cooked, David brought fuel and Stephen brought some water with Becky's help. Johanna stayed with Almanzo, bathing him again and again. But still he wouldn't wake up. Her ma insisted she take a walk. She hadn't taken but a couple of steps when she saw Rick. He moved to take her in his arms but she shook her head.

"I don't know why Almanzo is still sleeping."

For a moment, she thought he was going to argue with her but he didn't. Instead he said, "I brought you something. Well, actually, Sarah wanted you to have it."

Johanna flushed with guilt. "I am so sorry. I haven't even asked you how she and Carrie are. I have been so caught up..."

"Jo, don't apologize. Sarah is alive thanks to you and both girls are fine. Sarah thought this might be able to help Almanzo."

Johanna opened the parcel. Inside was Sarah's favorite book about castles and princesses. Her throat choked up. She had to wipe her eyes too. She looked up at him to see concern and love reflected in his eyes.

"She didn't mean to make you cry. She also suggested that you change the princesses to princes or you may offend Almanzo."

"She is so sweet. Tell her thank you and I will come and see her as soon as I can. I don't want to see her now in case I make her sick again."

"Jo, I know why you are looking after the boy and I admire you for it. But..."

"But?"

"Just let others help. You are very tired after the last bought of illness. I don't want to lose you. If that makes me selfish then I am sorry."

She wrapped her arms around herself, holding the book close to her chest.

"If I wasn't afraid of being contagious I would hug you right now," she whispered.

He moved closer, putting his arms around her.

"I will take my chances."

He brought his lips down to meet hers. It was a firm but gentle kiss.

"You are a very special lady, Miss Thompson."

She lay her head on his chest, needing his strength.

"I best get back to the girls." His reluctance to leave her made her feel better.

"Tell them I will see them soon. And give Sarah an extra big cuddle for the book."

* * *

JOHANNA CLIMBED BACK into the wagon, checked on Almanzo before taking a seat and opening the book. Starting at page one she began to read, but mindful of Sarah's remark, she changed the story to fit that of a young prince. Every so often, she checked her patient, but if he heard the story or was aware she was there, he gave no sign.

A few hours later, Becky came in and more or less threw her out of the wagon.

"You have to sleep for a few hours. Captain Jones' orders. Now get. I will come and get you if he wakes."

Johanna wanted to argue with her sister but she didn't have the energy. She climbed down from the wagon as quietly as possible so as not to disturb her ma and pa who were asleep underneath. Then she made her way into the tent, where without bothering to change she lay down. She was asleep almost before her head hit the pillow.

CHAPTER 33

The next few days passed pretty much the same as before. Almanzo's fever broke and stayed down but he did not recover consciousness.

"Maybe he hit his head and there are internal injuries we cannot see?"

"Perhaps, Johanna, or maybe he just doesn't want to wake up," Ma said. She'd helped Johanna change the young boy's position in the makeshift bed.

"Why wouldn't he want to wake up?" Johanna asked, not trying to hide her disbelief.

Her ma put an arm around her shoulders. "Sometimes life can be very painful, Johanna. We don't fully understand the body and mind. Maybe by letting him sleep, God is allowing him to build up his strength to deal with his new... situation."

Johanna looked from the unconscious child to her ma and back again. Maybe her ma was right. But she really wished Almanzo would wake up. Only when she heard him speak would she stop worrying about him.

"Him waking up won't stop you worrying. If anything, you will worry more."

"How do you know exactly what I am thinking?" Johann asked in a bemused tone.

"'Cause I am your ma. Now leave me to watch him for a while. You need to eat and look after yourself. I also think you should do some visiting."

"Visiting?" Johanna's cheeks warmed as she tried to busy herself around the tiny space in the wagon.

"Yes, dear. There is a certain young man who would benefit from seeing you. Now don't go pretending you don't know whom I am speaking about. But have a wash first, darling. The wagon is stifling."

Johanna grinned at her mother. She was lucky to have such wonderful parents.

She had a quick wash and then changed her dress and rebraided her hair before making her way to see Rick and the girls. Carrie saw her first and came running toward her.

"Jo, we missed you. Are you coming to see us?"

"Yes, Carrie, I missed you too. How are you? How is Sarah?"

The girl's mouth turned down. "She's back to normal. She was shouting at me earlier."

Johanna laughed. "You missed her doing that. You told me remember?"

Carrie grinned up at her. "I guess I did but now I don't think I meant it."

They held hands until they reached the wagon where Sarah was waiting.

"Would you like some coffee, Jo? I made it and Uncle Rick says it's not too bad."

"I would love some, thank you, Sarah. You look so much better."

"I am, thanks to you and Uncle Rick."

Johanna sat wondering where Rick was but she didn't want the girls to think she had only come to see him.

"Uncle Rick had to go over to the Freeman's. Sheila came over earlier to say her pa was worried about one of his tires. It looked as if it was loose."

Johanna almost gasped out loud at the twinge of jealousy she felt over Rick going to help Sheila. Of course he would do that. Just as he would go to the aid of Mrs. Newland or anyone else.

"Jo, how is Almanzo? Are we allowed to visit him yet?"

"In a couple of days. He is getting better but is still

very tired."

"Is it true, he was left there alone?" Sarah whispered probably hoping her younger sister wouldn't hear her.

"We don't know anything for sure yet. So tell me your news. Have you been doing your reading, Carrie?"

"Yes, ma'am. Sarah said I am getting better. Didn't you?" Carrie looked up at her big sister for confirmation.

"She is. She is working so hard. Ma would be very proud of her."

Johanna choked up at the look of love the girls exchanged. While they had always been close despite the fact they bickered, there seemed to be a new depth to the relationship between them. She spent a while with them, taking turns to listen to Carrie's reading and then reading them a bedtime story.

"I better get back to my wagon. Goodnight, girls."

"Goodnight, Jo. Uncle Rick will be sorry he missed you."

"No doubt I will see him around tomorrow."

Johanna walked slowly back to her wagon and was almost there when suddenly hands grabbed her, pulling her behind one of the wagons.

"I thought I would never get away. I've missed you."

"Rick, you almost gave me a heart attack."

"Is that why your heart is racing? I thought you were just pleased to see me."

She was about to protest but as she looked up at him, her eyes focused on his lips. She leaned up on her toes and kissed him.

"I am."

"Show me."

She kissed him again, this time using her lips to explore his. His hands moved up her back, one playing with her hair while another caressed the back of her neck. She closed the distance between them as their kiss deepened. Her heart raced as her breathing quickened. Panting she pulled away, laying her head on his shoulder.

"You are so beautiful and you smell so good. I thought I was never going to see you. I came to the wagon a couple of times but you were so busy with Almanzo. How is he?"

Tears sprang into Johanna's eyes.

"He is so hurt, he cannot even talk to me. He won't admit they left him behind to die. I can't believe it but Captain Jones said he had proof."

"Jones is an honest man."

"Yes, but how could any parent leave their own child like that? He's only a young boy not an animal."

Rick pulled her closer as she wept out her fears for Almanzo on his shoulder.

"I can't bear the thought of him being left alone."

"Will he not continue to travel with your folks?"

"Yes, of course, but I meant when we get to Oregon. I don't know if my parents will want to keep him. Another boy on top of Stephen might prove too much for them."

"Don't worry about that now. We won't let him be alone. I promise."

He bent down to kiss her, this time the kiss full of reassurance. She clung to him taking strength from his embrace.

"I best get back. Ma will wonder where I am."

"Goodnight, sweetheart. Promise me you will look after yourself."

She blew him a kiss and walked quickly back to the wagon. There she met her ma.

"Looks like that visit cheered you up some."

"Yes, Ma, thank you. How is Almanzo?"

"He's sleeping. Now get to bed Johanna. You won't be good to man or beast if you keep burning the candle at both ends."

"Night, Ma."

"Sweet dreams, darling."

CHAPTER 34

"Y ou are awake." Johanna beamed at the small boy who looked even younger than his ten years. He had lost a lot of weight. But that wasn't her concern. The lack of interest in his eyes hurt her. She wanted to gather him close to her and tell him how much he was loved. But she couldn't move. She sensed he wouldn't welcome her embrace—not yet.

"Yes, I woke up a while ago. Why am I traveling in your wagon?"

"You have been very ill."

"But why your wagon?"

Johanna wasn't sure how to answer the child. Did he remember anything? Was he testing her?

"Almanzo what do you remember?"

"About what?"

"Being ill?"

"I remember Pa leaving the wagon train with the others. Your family was sick and you had to stay behind." Almanzo lay on his side, his head resting on his elbow. "Ma and Pa argued a lot about it. Ma wanted to stay but Pa said we had to think about our future. We traveled for some hours before people started slowing down. They were sick too. Pa got very angry."

"Was your Pa ill?"

"No, he wasn't. Ma was but he told her she had to keep going. We couldn't stop or we would get caught in the snows. You know like the people in those stories."

Johanna didn't want to think about them. "So how did you come to us? Did you come to find help?"

Almanzo lay back down on the covers. "I am tired. Can we talk later."

"Yes, of course, you rest. I will come back when the wagon stops again. I have filled the water bottle beside you."

"Thank you, Jo." His voice skipped slightly.

She pretended not to notice the tears that slipped out of his closed eyes. She forced herself to sound cheerful.

"You woke up on the best day. Mr. Clarke and Mr. Hughes found some buffalo yesterday. A young cow so the meat will be tender."

There was no response. Johanna climbed down from

the wagon carefully. Her pa wasn't driving fast but still she didn't want to have an accident.

* * *

"Captain Jones wants us to keep traveling today and not stop at noon. He said to make extra food at breakfast. He's concerned about the lack of wood around. Ideally, we want to find an area of wood and good grass and water."

"Not asking for much, is he?" Ma asked, smiling.

It was so nice to see her ma and pa smiling again. Johanna didn't have any reply. She trusted Captain Jones to do what was best for them. He hadn't failed them yet. And if they kept moving, she could avoid the conversation she knew she would have to have with Almanzo.

They finally found a campsite providing much of what Captain Jones had wanted. The water was slightly warm but not unpleasant tasting. As they were setting up the fire, the children came running over.

"Jo, look. There's lots of them. Come pick them with us, please."

The children ran around Johanna showing her the black currants they had already picked.

"Go with them, dear. Maybe I can make a cobbler later."

"Ma, you need to rest. We can eat them as they are. They will be a nice change from dried apple."

Becky and Milly came with them, and together they picked a wonderful amount of berries. There would be enough for everyone. The children came back with their mouths covered in purple juice. Rick Hughes burst out laughing as the girls ran up to him.

"Look, Uncle Rick, I got lots and lots," Carrie said beaming up at him.

"You look as if you each ate half a bush," he said teasingly, his eyes greeting Johanna warmly.

"You look better today, Miss Thompson. I hope you are feeling well."

"Yes, thank you."

"How is your patient?"

"He is improving. He may be able to walk a little bit tomorrow."

"Did he like my book?"

"Yes, Sarah, darling, he loved it. But I did have to follow your advice and change the princesses into princes."

"Yeah, boys don't like princesses."

"Now I wouldn't say that, Sarah. Most men want to treat their lady like a princess but often the lady won't let them." Johanna couldn't look at him as he spoke to his niece. She knew he was talking about her. Hadn't her ma said something similar? About letting a man help a woman out. She should be less independent but she wasn't sure she knew how.

* * *

LATER WHEN THEY set up camp, Rick called to check on Almanzo.

"Sarah was wondering if she could come and visit with Almanzo. But I said I would check with you first. I don't want Sarah becoming ill again."

Johanna pulled at Rick's arm to get his attention before gesturing they should walk.

"I didn't want Almanzo to hear me."

"Pity, I thought you just wanted to be alone with me." He waggled his eyebrows at her making her laugh. His kiss drove away all thoughts of laughter. When they finally broke apart, she had to wait a couple of seconds for her pulse to stop racing.

"What was I saying?"

"I don't know. If I kiss you again, maybe you will remember?"

She smiled up at him. "Kissing you makes me forget everything. You are a total distraction."

He rubbed his chin pretending to be insulted. "Well, I guess I've been called worse." He touched her face tenderly. "You wanted to tell me something Almanzo couldn't hear."

"Poor boy. He is getting better and is no danger to Sarah. What he has, she can't catch."

"What do you mean?"

"Oh, Rick, he's brokenhearted. You should see the look in his eyes. He cries when he thinks nobody can hear him. I just want to cuddle him but something about him stops me. I wish I could reach him."

"He must have got a real fright. Alone and ill, not to mention wondering about his parents."

"That's the key. I think he remembers them leaving, but he just won't talk about it. He won't eat and doesn't seem to care whether we make progress or not. He just lies there. He's wasting away right before my eyes."

"You got to force him to talk to you. You can do it. If anyone can. People trust you. You got to trust yourself."

"I don't know how to handle his hurt. Or his questions about the future. What can I promise him? I know nothing of Oregon."

"You can do the same for him as you did for Sarah and Carrie. Show him he is loved and will never be alone. That's all you can do. You will never take the place of his parents, but you can show him people care about him. What did you say to me? Children can get over most things if they know they are loved."

She smiled at him ruefully as he used her own words to persuade her.

"Come here."

She obeyed his softly spoken order as she moved into his arms. He held her tight, caressing the top of her head. "I never met anyone with a heart as pure as yours. You can do this, I know you can."

She looked up into his eyes, the strength of his feelings taking her breath away. Reaching up on her tippy toes she dragged his head towards hers, her lips meeting his with a burning intensity. She loved him desperately and wanted to show him just how much. He returned her kiss, pushing her gently backwards until she was resting against a tree. His hands moved around her back before lingering at her waist as his mouth explored hers. She completely forgot about everything apart from the feel of his body next to hers. For a couple of precious minutes, they could put aside all their worries and just enjoy being with one another under the starry evening sky.

CHAPTER 35

The next evening, Almanzo got up and walked around the camp site, leaning on Johanna's arm. He was weak so she didn't let him go far. He sat on a stone beside the fire. Everyone else seemed to have business elsewhere. Johanna knew they were giving her space to speak to the boy in private.

"Did you enjoy the story from Sarah's book?"

Almanzo nodded. Johanna wasn't sure how to get him speaking but she had to try.

"Sarah is an orphan, isn't she?" Almanzo asked surprising Johanna.

"She probably is. We don't know for definite. Her pa hasn't been heard from in some time."

"What will she do when she goes to Oregon? Is she and her sister going to live with Mr. Hughes?"

"That's the plan. Why?"

"Just asking."

Johanna's heart almost missed a beat. She saw his questions for what they really were.

"Are you worried about what you will do?" she asked him quietly. When he didn't answer, she prompted, "In Oregon."

"I'll find something. I can work on a farm. I did it before."

"Almanzo, what happened to your parents?"

His eyes closed but not before she saw his pain. She moved closer to him.

"Tell me. Please."

"They left."

Johanna forced herself to stay quiet. It wasn't the time to badger him with questions.

"They argued. Ma didn't want to go but Pa made her. I was ill. Ma said I could travel in the wagon, but Pa said I would make them all sick. He left me with the others."

"Others?"

"Most people who left with my pa got sick. We all drank the same water. I guess it was bad. Some died and we buried them but then more got sick. Every morning it was worse. Ma was ill but she got better. Pa wasn't feeling too good either else he would have left earlier. But then he recovered so he said he was leaving. I tried telling him what he was doing wasn't right. Some of the other men argued, too, but he wouldn't listen. When I woke up in the morning, he was gone."

Johanna couldn't resist. She pulled the boy toward her. He stiffened at first before the dam burst and the tears came. Her own tears flooded her face, falling on his hair.

"My poor boy. Nothing like that will ever happen to you again. You will never be left alone."

"But when we get to Oregon... your family have plans."

"They will include you. I swear to you, Almanzo. If we find your parents and you want to go back to them, that will be your choice. But you will always have a home with me."

He stared at her as if he didn't believe her.

"She's right, son, nobody will ever leave you to live alone again."

Both of them jumped as Rick Hughes joined them at the fireside.

Almanzo rubbed his sleeve across his face, leaving Johanna wishing she could do the same. Rick gave her hand a squeeze.

"You are part of Captain Jones' team and we all stick together, like glue," Rick said. "You will have chores to do though."

"I will work harder than anyone else, Mr...." Almanzo faltered.

Johanna guessed he couldn't remember Rick's name.

"My name is Rick Hughes, lad. You don't have to worry about working harder than anyone else. Just do your best. That's all we can ask."

Johanna hugged herself as Almanzo had moved away from her side once Rick arrived.

"Now, Almanzo, do you think you could go to bed? I have something I want to talk to Miss Thompson about."

"Yes, sir. Goodnight."

"Come back here, Almanzo." Johanna stood up and gave the boy a hug. "I want you to be happy and remember you are safe with us."

"Yes, Jo. I know." He hugged her back before half walking half running back to the wagon to his bed.

"Thank you for coming to find us."

"Was it as bad as you feared?" he asked her, taking her hand in his.

She lay her head on his shoulder. "Much worse," she said softly.

He held her close as she cried not just for Almanzo, but for the other victims. They knew the trail would be hard but nobody had warned them of man's potential cruelty to their fellow passengers.

They didn't get a chance to talk in private as Becky arrived followed closely by Stephen.

"Evening, Mr. Hughes. How is Almanzo?" Becky asked as if having Rick at their fire was an everyday occurrence.

"He was tired so went to bed. Please thank Sarah again for the book."

"I will. Goodnight, Miss Thompson. Stephen."

Johanna watched as Rick walked away wondering what he had wanted to speak to her about. She caught Becky's smile.

"Good job it was us and not Ma and Pa who came back early," Becky teased.

Johanna didn't reply. She didn't have the energy. Between Rick's presence and Almanzo's revelations she felt emotionally drained and very, very tired.

"I am going to turn in. Goodnight, Stephen, Becky."

She didn't wait for their reply but hurried to the tent. In fairness, Becky gave her the space she needed. Her twin remained sitting at the fire for some time.

CHAPTER 36

The next few days, traveling was extremely frustrating for both animals and humans. The animals bellowed crossly as they could smell the water below but couldn't reach it. The view from the mountain down to the water was amazing, as were the few waterfalls they came across, but not having access to the cool refreshment made traveling stressful. The dust was a problem and soon everyone—even those with the most cheerful dispositions—was miserable.

* * *

IT WAS Johanna's turn to drive the wagon. She didn't usually mind but the mountain trail made her slightly nervous.

"I'm taking over." Rick Hughes came riding up beside her.

"You can't drive all the wagons over."

"Jo, there is a very long and steep hill up ahead. It will be a challenge for even the most experienced driver."

"I can do it," she vowed, not sure if she was trying to convince him or herself. Captain Jones rode up to them.

"There is no way the wagon will make it down that hill alone. You need to lock both rear wagon wheels. Hughes and I will ride at the back to hold the wagon wheels."

"You can't mean her to drive?" Rick asked, an incredulous look on his face.

"I wouldn't, usually, but with her pa and Clarke still weak from being ill, there is no one else. Becky, I mean Miss Thompson is driving the Long wagon as I need Jessie to help get us down."

"I will be fine," Jo insisted, trying to quell the knots in her stomach. "Look at it this way, the sooner we get to the valley the better. We will have fresh water and grass for the animals. Everyone will feel better."

Captain Jones tipped his hat at her before riding away. She guessed he had gone to check on Becky. Rick Hughes stayed on his horse staring at her.

"What?" Jo asked, arching an eyebrow.

"I can't make up my mind if you are brave or foolhardy. Have you any idea how dangerous this is?"

"Stop shouting. Do you want to cause a panic? I am not stupid, *Mr.* Hughes." She was angry, he seemed to think she was foolhardy. "Of course I realize the danger, but the reality is there is no other choice."

He stared at her as if he was going to answer but changed his mind. She knew he was worried but she was still angry he thought she might be taking a risk for the sake of it.

"Jo?"

"Yes," she replied without looking up from the reins gripped so tight between her fingers, her knuckles had turned white.

"Be careful."

She looked at him, seeing the concern in his eyes. "I will," she said softly. "You take care too."

He nodded before nudging his horse and riding slowly to the back of the wagon where Captain Jones was waiting.

* * *

JOHANNA LOOKED DOWN at the road in front of her. It was such a sheer drop, she wasn't at all sure she would be able to control the wagon. But she had to give it her best shot. Ma and Pa were walking down with some of the other folk. It would be hard on them but slightly safer than riding in the wagon. Almanzo was still in the back where David Clark had helped her to build him a nest surrounded by feather beds. She hoped it would protect him a little from the jolting. There was no other way, he was too frail to walk that far.

She spoke to the oxen softly wondering if they were afraid too. She didn't think so as they seemed content to nibble at some grass along the side of the trail. She promised them oats with molasses if they got her down in one piece.

"Let's move out."

That was the signal. Johanna was ready or at least she thought she was but the actual reality was more difficult than she imagined. The pull on the wagon to move forward at a fast speed was so strong she had difficulty restraining the oxen even with the back wheels locked. She risked a glance over her shoulder but she couldn't see the two men who strained to hold the wagon steady from behind. She brushed the sweat from her brow with her sleeve not wanting to release the reins even for one second. She wished her hat did more to protect her eyes. It kept the worst of the sun off her head but her eyes were sore. Still, they were moving and there was no going back. She had to succeed for everyone's sake. If the wagon fell, not only would it drag her and Almanzo to almost certain death, but it would also place Rick and Captain Jones in jeopardy too.

In some places, she actually closed her eyes, not wanting to stare at the steep drop in front of her. Why couldn't they have found a better route? Surely the people who had traveled before them would have carved out a safer road? But even as the thoughts ran through her mind she knew she was following in the exact trail of countless travelers before her. She kept her eyes on the road trying to block out the broken wagons and other signs of those emigrants who hadn't been successful. She had to move forward. There was no other way.

Although it seemed to take forever, it was soon over. Everyone cheered as the wagon safely arrived. Relieved the trip was over, Johanna didn't get much chance to celebrate as she realized Rick and Captain Jones had returned back up the mountain in order to help the next wagon down. It was a long and agonizing wait. Finally, all ten of the caravans left in their group had made their way down safely.

"Oh, Johanna, I never want to do that again. I don't care if Oregon is the most horrid place on earth. I am never leaving. I don't want to face this trip again—ever."

Johanna held the tearful Milly until she regained her

composure. Over her shoulder, she exchanged a look with Rick. In his eyes, she saw relief and also pride. He was proud of her. Maybe the trip down the mountain had been worth it after all.

CHAPTER 37

*J*ohanna looked ahead at the steam rising from the pools of water. It was an amazing sight. The water boiled out right from the ground forming fountains in some places. There was a funny smell, not unpleasant but she wasn't sure she liked it either. She hoped Captain Jones would let them stop and have a bath. The thoughts of having a warm bath had kept her going over the last few days when the traveling had been particularly hard and dusty.

"This is the famous soda springs? Is it true the water tastes like real soda?" Stephen came racing up to her, followed closely behind by Carrie.

"Don't drink any yet, Stephen. Wait until I taste it first."

"That's not fair. Why do you get some?"

"Johanna is looking after you. She doesn't want you to get sick."

"I won't, Ma. I am as strong as an ox." Stephen ran off. Jo went to follow him but her ma put her hand on her arm to stop her.

"Let him go. Won't do him any harm."

"But what if he gets a bellyache?"

"Then he may listen to his older sister." Her ma's eyes twinkled.

Johanna gave her an impulsive hug pleased to see her ma's spirit had returned.

"I am very proud of my three daughters. You girls saw us through the bad times back there. Your pa is too, although I am not sure he will ever put it into words."

Tears pricked Johanna's eyes as she thought of just how close she had come to losing her precious ma and pa. If this trail had taught them anything, it was family was more important than anything.

"Thanks, Ma. Don't go overdoing it now though. You gave us all quite a scare," she said in a husky voice.

"I won't. Now go find that nice Mr. Hughes and ask him to help you get some water."

"I can get that, Ma. Becky will help me."

Her words led to her ma rolling her eyes.

"Johanna Thompson, go act like a maiden in distress and let that man you've set your heart on rescue you.

After these past few days fending for yourself and being so strong, I imagine he is a little in awe of you."

"Ma!" Johanna protested but at her ma's fixed stare, she said, "Do you really think I should?"

"Yes, but fix your hair before you go. You look like a bee's nest took root in it."

Johanna decided she would seek out a bath before she looked for Rick. Her hair was thick with dust and she couldn't wait to soap it all off. The other women had a similar plan and soon there was a group of them giggling like school girls as they sought out a private spot. The water was even more heavenly than she had imagined. The pains and aches in her bones soothed away as she lay in the relaxing waters.

"I could stay here forever," Becky said as she soaped up her hair.

"You would end up looking like a prune," Milly teased, sitting by the side of the pool. She didn't want to risk getting in. Nobody knew if the water was safe for a pregnant woman so she'd decided not to take the chance. Johanna and Becky had washed her hair so at least that was clean.

"Look at the men. You would think they knew better."

They looked into the distance to see the men trying to sit on top of one of the springs. The force of the water was throwing them off but they kept returning for another go.

"I can see why they call it steamboat springs. It sounds just like the steamboat that used to go up and down the river at home," Mrs. Newland commented. "Never thought I would see grown men behave like children." Although she tutted, Johanna got the merry glint in her eye. The older woman approved of the men forgetting their cares for a while.

"Looks like it's true. They may grow older but they don't grow up," Eva said, smiling at their antics.

"They are just blowing off steam. After the events of the last few weeks who can blame them." Gracie's sad tone as she put her own thoughts into words made Johanna want to hug her. Her friend had put on a little of the weight she'd lost when ill but her love of life hadn't returned. She wondered if it ever would.

"Life goes on Gracie. We have to believe there are good times waiting for us ahead." Although Sheila's tone was gruff, Johanna saw her squeezing Gracie's hand in support.

"Almanzo looks like he is enjoying himself," Becky said watching the group in the distance. The young boy was lying in the water laughing at the antics of the men. He hadn't made any move to join them. Johanna wasn't worried as she knew it would take time to build his strength back up after his ordeal.

"Jo, can you come, please?" Carrie shouted, running toward them.

"What's the matter?"

"It's Stephen. He says his belly is going to burst. Is it? It's all round and he's crying," Carrie said miserably.

"He's just drank too much of the soda water. Jo told him not to but looks like he didn't listen," Becky said, not moving from the water.

"Will he die?" Carrie's big blue eyes seemed to take over her face.

"No, honey, he won't but he is likely to have a belly-ache for a while." Johanna was quick to reassure her. The little girl had seen enough death for a lifetime.

Carrie's expression changed as she stamped her foot. "You mean he knew he would be sick but he drank it anyway."

Johanna had to try very hard not to laugh. "Yes, honey."

"Wait till I get my hands on him," Carrie shouted racing away.

The women all giggled. "The start of a beautiful new romance," Milly suggested causing more laughter.

Johanna had a feeling her brother's ears might soon

hurt more than his belly but it was all he deserved. She wasn't worried enough to stop bathing.

* * *

It was a long time before she followed her ma's advice and went to find Rick. She couldn't ask him to find water for her given they were surrounded by it. That would be too obvious. She was still thinking of an excuse when he interrupted her musings.

"Hello. You look lovely."

His compliment and the look in his eyes got her all flustered. Her heart was racing as her stomach twisted into knots. "Thank you," she finally managed. "How are the girls? Did they enjoy the soda?"

"Not as much as your Stephen from what Carrie told me. She is quite cross with him."

Johanna giggled making Rick smile. "It's lovely to see you looking so happy."

"I had a wonderful day."

"It was nice of you to come check on the girls. Would you like some coffee?"

Tongue tied, Johanna could only nod. What could she ask him to do to help her? Racking her brains, she drew to a dead end. Then she spotted his wagon.

"Pa thought he might have damaged a wheel when

we went over a hole a few miles back. Would you mind having a look at it?"

He looked surprised, as he should, given that her pa or David would have more expertise with wagon wheels than he did.

"Sure, I can take a look." He stared at her. "Does your pa know you asked me?"

"No. But I am certain he'd appreciate the help." She wasn't at all sure but what could she say. Why didn't she think of something different? Oh wait till she saw her ma. She'd have a thing or two to say about pretending to be a damsel in distress.

"Will we take a look now?"

She nodded, afraid to say anything as her stomach churned. What would her pa say if Rick suddenly wanted to inspect his wheels? He wasn't known for his subtlety.

She walked back to the wagon in silence. Rick seemed to pick up on her discomfort as his initial burst of conversation waned. She looked around quickly but couldn't see her pa. Maybe he had gone to visit Mr. Bradley or one of his other friends.

"See, it's that wheel there. Does it look different to you?"

Rick studied the wheel for so long Johanna was fit to burst. Just how much longer would it take him to say there was nothing wrong with the wagon wheel. Pa would be back soon if she didn't hurry him up.

"I guess it looks okay?" She prompted.

"I don't rightly know. Seems a bit bent to me," Rick replied, his voice sounding funny.

"Bent? How can a wheel be bent?" She peered down at the wheel as she asked. She didn't see him move toward her until he had his arms at her waist. She jumped as his hands made contact with her skin.

"I think it looks a little funny from this angle and maybe this one as well." He kissed her lightly making her move slightly to the left and to the right. Her stomach went into free-fall. He knew she'd made the whole thing up. How embarrassing. What was she going to do or say now? She looked into his eyes and saw his desire for her. All embarrassment faded as she gave herself up to his kiss.

Thank goodness her ma called out before her parents arrived back at the wagon. Rick jumped away from her, almost turning the pot on the camp fire over in his haste.

"That you, Johanna, making such a racket?"

"Sorry, Pa, I didn't see the pot." Johanna hoped her voice sounded less strained to her pa's ears. She could feel Rick's body shake as he laughed behind her. Thankful for the darkness, she pushed him away. The last thing she wanted was for her pa to find them alone. Rick stole another kiss and then he was gone.

"You making coffee? I could do with a cup after all your ma's chatting."

"Me? You never stopped talking from the minute you came to find me."

Johanna let her parents' chatter go over her head. She was too busy trying to calm herself. Her ma cast her a curious look but she didn't say anything. Johanna made some excuse and almost ran to the tent where Becky was trying to read. She gave up the minute Johanna arrived.

"What happened to you? You're all red."

"I caught too much sun today."

"That's not the sun. You saw Rick, didn't you? Did he kiss you so much your toes turned up?" Becky laughed at her own joke but when Johanna didn't respond, she sat up in her bedroll. "He did kiss you. Oh, this is so exciting. You like him a lot, don't you?"

Johanna didn't trust herself to speak so simply nodded.

"He likes you too. It's obvious from the way he looks at you. Is he going to speak to Pa?"

"No. I don't know. He hasn't said anything about the future." But he did tell her he loved her. She wasn't going to share that with Becky. She loved her sister but given her inclination to be impulsive, she didn't trust her not to say something to Ma or worse to their pa.

"He will. Just give him time."

"What about you? Have you had a chance to spend time with Captain Jones yet?"

"Alone? Are you joking? It would be easier to climb the bluffs in a skirt than catch that man alone. Honestly, why does everyone have to run to him with the smallest of problems?"

Johanna sympathized with Becky but it was part of his job.

"Well, Ma would say absence makes the heart fonder. You will have his full attention when we reach Oregon."

"I aim to have it long before then. Goodnight." Becky lay back down, a catlike smile on her face.

Johanna changed for bed not wanting to ask Becky what she had planned. Sometimes it was best not knowing.

* * *

THE NEXT MORNING, her ma called her to help with making some bread.

"Mrs. Newland says the water will help it rise. She heard it from a friend of hers who traveled to Oregon some years back."

Johanna didn't much care. Her mind revolved around Rick. Why hadn't he made any mention of the future?

"So I take it from the look on your face last night, things went well with Mr. Hughes?"

"Ma. Don't be asking me questions like that."

"Why not? You are my daughter and I want you to be happy. From what I can see, Mr. Hughes is a fine man. He has taken responsibility for those nieces of his. That's a lot for a single young man." Ma turned her attention back to the bread. "You like him, don't you?"

"Yes, Ma."

"And he likes you. That much is obvious. Has he mentioned anything about talking to your pa? You know your father is very traditional."

"Yes, Ma, I know. Rick, I mean Mr. Hughes hasn't mentioned Pa. We haven't discussed the future." Johanna's cheeks could have cooked the bread. She wanted to escape but she didn't want to risk upsetting her ma either.

"That will come in time. For now, allow yourself some time to get to know each other. Plenty of time for serious courting when we get to Oregon."

"Do you think everyone will settle near each other?"

Ma rubbed the hair from her eyes leaving a trail of flour on her face. "I hope so, darling, as I have grown very fond of our fellow travelers. But we shall have to see. There is plenty of ground to cover before we reach our final destination."

Johanna heard the fear behind those words but she didn't comment on it. They all knew the dangers ahead, the most difficult terrain had yet to be crossed. But it was senseless dwelling on what could happen. All they could do was take each day as it came.

"You go on now, girl. I have this in hand."

"Thanks, Ma." Johanna ran before her ma could change her mind. It was all very well her mother was in favor of a match, but it was another thing discussing her feelings for Rick. They were so new and exciting, she wanted to savor them before having to share with anyone else.

* * *

"Yuck. How can there be so many of them? It's like the locust plague in the bible."

"Don't be so dramatic, Becky, it is only a few crickets."

"Eva Thompson Clarke, you come over here and tell me this is a few of those horrible creatures. Look around you. They are everywhere."

The girls looked at the ground. It was a heaving mass

of black insects with bulging eyes and no wings. They had never seen anything like them before. They were still staring at them as Captain Jones rode up.

"I see you have found our latest trial. Previous travelers called them Mormon crickets but I don't know why. I do know the local Indians add these insects to soups, they swear it makes for a healthy nutritious meal."

Becky glanced at her sisters, their faces sharing her own distaste at the thoughts of eating the disgusting things.

"Are they dangerous? Do they bite?"

"Not you but they will eat much everything else. Crops, quilts, linens, clothes, even their own kind. You should make sure your packed dry goods are properly sealed."

Eva and Johanna moved to follow his instructions, but Becky stayed where she was. She wasn't about to waste the opportunity of spending a little time alone with him, insects or no insects.

"Apart from the insects, are you well?"

"I am fine, thank you. How do you know so much about the local Indians?" She was immediately sorry she had asked. His eyes held a mixture of pain, and was it fear? What could he be afraid of?

"It's a wagon master's job to know about those who live on the trail."

"Are they dangerous?"

"Not usually."

His tone suggested he didn't want to discuss Indians. Becky was tempted to ask why but she reluctantly remembered her promise to behave like a lady.

"Pa says we will soon reach Fort Hall."

"Yes, day after tomorrow if we keep this pace up. It will be a good chance to restock supplies, particularly of medications. However, if you think the crickets are ugly, wait until you see the mosquitoes. I don't think I have ever seen so many in one place."

Becky grinned up at him. "Well, seeing as you paint such a pretty picture, I can't wait to experience it."

He burst out laughing at her response. She walked back to their camp pleased she had made him laugh. She could feel his eyes on her but she resisted the temptation to look back. She had to make him want her as much as she wanted him.

* * *

"We will reach Fort Hall later this afternoon."

"Do you remember how excited you were about the dance at the first fort we visited when we started out? I seem to remember you wanted to stay and live with Captain Wilson."

"Stop teasing, Ma. You know I wasn't really interested in him."

"Who might I ask are you interested in? Not our own Captain Jones, I hope."

Becky's heart missed a beat. It had never crossed her mind that her parents might not approve of Scott.

"Would that be a problem?"

"Becky, your pa and I want you to be happy." Ma didn't look her in the eyes making her stomach grow tighter.

"But?" she prompted.

"Captain Jones is years older than you and he has a...past."

"Of course he has a past. We all do. That doesn't matter. What matters is he is brave and strong and caring and wonderful. I love him, Ma."

"You don't know him, not really." Ma held her hand up to stop Becky from speaking. "I am not saying he isn't a good man. He is. I admire him and believe he has many excellent qualities. But we don't feel he is the right man for you, Becky. He has a wanderlust."

"What does that mean?"

"Darling, he isn't going to be happy settling in one

place. People like Captain Jones thrive on danger. They like traveling from one place to the next."

"Ma, you make him sound like an Indian." The look on her ma's face made her nervous. It wasn't that she was shocked, in fact, she looked like she was hiding something. Becky decided it was time for a different tactic. "But you are right. I am only seventeen and I want to see a little of the world before I tie myself to any man."

The relief on her ma's face almost made her cry out in pain. What could her ma hold against Scott?

"I am so glad to hear that, Becky. Now why don't you find Johanna and check what supplies we need at the fort. I am going to check on Milly. She looked rather pale earlier." Her ma turned to go before she added, "Make sure you change before you go into the fort. I am not having my daughter walking around that place in pants and a shirt."

"Yes, Ma." Becky almost choked on the lump in her throat. She'd thought her biggest obstacle was getting Scott to see she was a grown woman. She had assumed her ma and pa would accept their relationship. Obviously, that wasn't the case. But it wouldn't matter. She was still going to marry Scott whether her ma liked it or not. She loved him too much to let him go for any reason. Her parents would come around to the idea eventually and if they didn't, then that would be their decision.

"You and Ma looked deep in discussion. What did she say to make you so cross?"

"Nothing, Jo."

Johanna looked at her in disbelief, but Becky refused to say another word. Her twin took the hint and soon they were discussing what supplies they needed at the fort. Contrary to her ma's opinion, Becky had been looking forward to seeing the fort but not anymore. The sooner they got to Oregon the better as far as she was concerned.

Becky had intended on going to the fort dressed as she was but then decided it was better not to incur her ma's wrath. Reluctantly, she traded her pants for a calico dress and female underthings. Johanna insisted on doing her hair.

"Captain Jones won't be able to take his eyes off you. I can't believe you are the same person. You look so beautiful in the dress."

Becky glanced in the small mirror Ma had brought along on the trip. She did look better in the dress, and Johanna had done a lovely job on her hair. Apart from her rather tanned complexion and slightly slender frame, she looked almost as she had done back in Virgil. But she was no longer the same empty-headed female.

Experiencing the trials of the journey so far had changed everyone. She wondered fleetingly what Ben, the banker's son, would think of her now. Somehow, she didn't think he would be interested in the new Becky. That suited her fine though. She only had eyes for one man. Captain Scott Jones.

CHAPTER 38

*E*va took Becky's elbow as they wandered around the fort. There were a lot of fur traders but also a lot of Indians. Too many eyes followed them, adding to the discomfort caused by the mosquitos. Scott hadn't been lying when he said she had never seen as many as she would experience at the fort.

They hadn't been there very long when a man sauntered up to them.

"What brings you two fine ladies to Fort Hall? Passing through or could you be persuaded to stay?"

Becky tried not to look sick as he spat brown tobacco juice from the side of his mouth covering his whiskers.

"Excuse me, sir, my husband is waiting for us."

The man ignored Eva's dismissive tone. "What about

you? You look a little young to be married? A couple of years, though, and you'd be mighty tasty." He put a hand out to touch a piece of her hair that had come loose from her braid. She pushed his hand away. "Don't touch me."

"You got spirit too. I like that in my women."

"Leave her alone, Mitchell, she wouldn't spit on your boots."

Becky was thrilled to hear Scott's voice.

"Thank you, Captain Jones. This *gentleman's* attentions are most unwelcome," Eva replied.

"Captain Jones? You consider him to be a gentleman? Standards must be very low where you are from, miss, particularly given he was living with the Indians for years. Got himself a squaw or two too. Perhaps that's what you like." The man took a step toward Eva and was rewarded for his efforts by a sharp kick from Becky's boot. At the same time, she pulled the small knife she always carried, not quite pointing it at him, but making sure he saw it all the same.

"Look, mister. My sister and I don't appreciate your disgusting talk. Now move along before I really get angry." Becky squared up to the man who took a step back in surprise. Captain Jones pushed Becky behind him, getting between them. "Mrs. Clarke, take Miss Thompson back to the wagon train. Now."

The two women walked quickly off. Becky didn't have much of a choice as Eva had a firm grip on her arm. She glanced behind her just in time to see Scott give the man a punch on the nose. "Eva, they are fighting. We should go back."

"We are going to do what Captain Jones told us. Becky Thompson, what did you think you were doing squaring up to a man like that? You could have been hurt."

"I wasn't letting him speak to you like that. I hate bullies."

"Sometimes I wonder if you were born in the wrong body. You behave worse than Stephen."

Becky didn't listen. Her sister would never understand her.

* * *

BECKY COULDN'T EAT dinner as she waited for Captain Jones to return to camp. Her parents had expressly forbidden her to go near the fort again. Eva had filled them in on what had happened, although she had kept the knife part to herself. Thankfully she also didn't mention the Indian squaw.

Her pa was beyond angry when he heard what the man had said. He wanted to go to the fort and hit the man himself but Ma made him promise to stay where he was.

Becky paced back and forward wishing she could change out of her dress but it would really annoy her ma. She wanted to go for a ride to work off her stress but that option was forbidden as well. Her pa insisted the area was too dangerous despite the presence of the soldiers. She kept thinking about the man, not because of what he had done but what he had said. He'd insinuated that not only had Scott lived with Indians, but he had married one. What type of man took an Indian bride? From what they had seen of the female members of the tribes, they weren't particularly attractive. Well, they might have been if they had been more inclined to wash and comb out their hair. Yet she sensed Scott had known the man. They certainly didn't behave like strangers.

She kept pacing as she gnawed at her lip. Did he have Indian children? Was his wife still alive? No, he wouldn't have kissed her if he was still married. He was an honorable man. Wasn't he?

She kicked at a stone. Her ma was right. She didn't know him, not really. In fact, they hadn't spent too much time talking. All they had done was argue and then make up. Despite herself, she sighed. She enjoyed kissing Scott. It was so different from the sweet, quick kisses she had exchanged with Ben and some of the other boys back in Virgil. But that was the difference. They had been boys, whereas Scott was a man with a past.

"You planning on planting seeds in that furrow you're making?"

His drawl drew her back to her senses. She fisted her hands hoping to keep her anger under control. Then she saw his face.

"You're hurt. What did he do to you?" She moved to examine his face but he stopped her.

"It's nothing. What the heck did you think you were doing standing up to a man like that? I have a good mind to give you a hiding right here."

"You keep threatening to spank me. Is that how you dealt with your squaw?" She bit her lip at the flare of pain in his eyes. She was angry but she hadn't meant to hurt him. "Scott, I'm sorry. I didn't…"

"Go to bed, Miss Thompson."

"I will not go to bed. I keep telling you I am not a child. What did that man mean? Do you have a wife? If so, what were you doing kissing me?"

"From what I recall, I wasn't the one doing the kissing."

She swung her hand at that remark, intent on hitting him. Instead he caught it and dragged her to him. He kissed her so intensely she thought she would combust. Her arms went around his neck as she encouraged his embrace. She'd been angry but also scared and needed his touch so badly. Her heart raced, matching the pulse quivering in his neck. He reluctantly released her mouth but held her close allowing both of them to recover.

"Becky, take a walk with me, please? I need to talk to you. I have to explain."

"You don't, at least not tonight. You need to go tend to your face or you will scare the children in the morning."

"But about that man, what he said?"

"He and his vile opinions are not worth my time. I trust you Scott Jones and that's all that matters to me. Now go on. Go fix that eye."

"Are you always going to be so unmanageable?"

Becky grinned. "Always."

He kissed her quickly on the lips before making his way in the direction of his own wagon. Becky walked quietly back to her tent, taking off her shoes to ensure nobody heard her. She didn't want to have to explain her disheveled hair to her parents.

CHAPTER 39

To everyone's relief they pulled out of camp the following morning. Nobody had enjoyed their visit to Fort Hall. It wasn't as much a reflection on the occupants of the fort as their warnings regarding the journey ahead. The wagon train turned west following the trail of emigrants before them who had traveled on to Oregon or California. The terrain became increasingly rough and the dangerously narrow bluffs made them all feel a little sick. They only made about ten miles a day. Captain Jones hadn't entertained any arguments about the pace simply telling them they would see the reason for the slow travel shortly. The stern, almost concerned look on his face prohibited anyone from teasing him over his black eye.

"Tomorrow, we will come to the American Falls.

Keep the children safe as the breathtaking beauty of roaring whitewater waterfalls is bound to fascinate them. If anyone falls in, there is no chance of rescue."

Johanna took his words to heart making sure all the children, particularly Stephen and Almanzo who were inclined to be more adventurous than the rest, stayed close.

* * *

WHEN THE GROUP set up camp that evening, Captain Jones called them together.

"The Indians around us are from the Shoshone tribe. They are usually friendly and peace loving people but tensions have been rising due to the number of emigrants crossing what they see as their land. Be pleasant but keep your wits about you. I recommend you trade for some fish. The salmon they catch has to be just about the nicest fish I have ever tasted."

Trading with the Indians was fun, but Becky couldn't help wondering if this was the tribe Scott had lived with. Johanna teased her for dreaming, but she kept looking at the women trying to see what a man like Jones would find attractive. These Indian women were gentle and kind, not in the least bit feisty like her. She traded a dress she particularly loathed for some moccasins and some fish.

Ma had suggested they all share a big meal rather than try to cook the fish over many different fires. Everyone agreed and there was a slightly festive air about the camp.

"Jones was right, this fish is incredible." Rick Hughes held his plate out for more. Becky watched as Johanna refilled his plate and gave his hand a quick squeeze. She looked toward their pa but he hadn't noticed anything. Her ma had, though, but judging by the smile on her face, she didn't mind. Her ma approved of Rick Hughes. He seemed like a nice man but Becky couldn't help feeling a little jealous. Why couldn't her ma approve of Scott too?

"Hughes, I've doubled the watch tonight."

"Why? I thought you said they were peaceful," Rick asked.

"They are but they can be mischievous. I would not put it past them to let some of the cattle out. Also, they are hungry, so they may take one or two of the cattle for meat. Either way, I am not taking any risks."

"We could spare a couple of the herd if they are that hungry. Especially as they are being so pleasant," David said. "They gave Eva a remedy for her mosquito bites. Don't smell too good but she says it's working already."

Becky smiled. Trust David to always suggest the nice thing to do. He was such a fair-minded man. She thought of the way he had smuggled food out to the slaves. He hated injustice in any form.

"Let's give them a couple of the older animals. They aren't as fussy as we are and the older ones are unlikely to last until Oregon anyway." Captain Jones suggested.

"But the meat is tough," Becky protested without thinking.

"To us it is. But the Indians have different methods of cooking. Their expectations are somewhat lower too." Her eyes met his as he was talking. She saw he was teasing her even if his words weren't that kind.

"I better get going. I want to put the girls to bed before I take up watch." Rick stood up, thanking her ma and the other ladies for a fine meal before he took his nieces off to bed. Ma shooed Stephen and Almanzo off too, as Becky got up to help her sisters tidy up. But Captain Jones stopped her. "Make sure you stay close to the wagons too. We aren't far enough yet from the fort for it to be safe."

"You don't think that man is coming after us, do you?"

"No, of course not." But his words lacked conviction.

"I..." At the look in his eyes, she realized he was

feeling the pressure of being responsible for all of them. "I promise to stay close. Don't worry."

"I wish I could but I can't help it," he whispered before walking away. Her pa came up behind her thus explaining Scott's sudden exit.

"What did Jones want?"

"He ordered all the women to stay close to the wagons. I am not sure he believes we are capable of looking after ourselves."

"It's the man's job to protect us, Rebecca. Don't you be reading more into his concern than that. You hear?"

"Yes, Pa." Becky hoped she sounded like a dutiful daughter. Now was not the time to try to convince her pa he was speaking about his future son-in-law.

CHAPTER 40

"How much longer will it take us to reach Oregon, Uncle Rick?"

"I don't know, Sarah, it depends on how far we travel every day." Rick wondered why Sarah was asking. "We are in Utah Territory now. Did you know that?"

"Yes, Johanna told us. She knows everything."

"You like her a lot, don't you?"

"Of course. She's nice. Don't you like her?"

"I like her."

"A lot?"

How was he supposed to answer that one? Johanna had crept into his heart but he wasn't going to admit that to his niece. At least not until he had asked Johanna to marry him. He didn't want to get the girls' hopes up in case she said no.

"Johanna seems sad sometimes," Sarah added. "I think she gets lonely."

"Why? She has her ma and pa, her sister and her brother to talk to."

He tried to find a way to distract Sarah. This wasn't a conversation he intended having with his niece.

"But it's not the same as having a prince, is it? When I grow up I am going to fall in love with a prince and live in a castle."

"Really? And where are you going to find this prince. We don't have princes in America."

"He'll find me. What's the name of that river?"

"That's the Snake River."

"It looks very fast."

"I guess it is but we have crossed rivers like it just fine. You don't need to worry. I won't let anything happen to you or your sister."

Sarah moved closer to him on the seat. "I know that, Uncle Rick. You are going to keep Carrie and me safe forever."

His heart clenched at the trust in her voice. He wished he could keep them safe forever, but what if their pa turned up? He had no legal right to the girls. What about his plans to leave them in an orphanage? He couldn't do that. Not anymore. They were no longer nieces he knew by name. Now they were real children with their own quirks and foibles. He couldn't love them more than if they were his own. Maybe he could adopt them. Would a court give him parental rights? He didn't know where Ellis was. But he had been gone two years so was that enough for abandonment.

"Uncle Rick, are you going to cross the river now? You are getting mighty close." Sarah's panic make him jerk the reins in time. He was too close to the river. The oxen must be thirsty to have come this near. He pulled on the reins, thankfully, they stopped. He hopped out giving the animals a quick drink so they didn't get any ideas about the river. Despite what he had said to Sarah, this was a dangerous river. Much more dangerous than the Platte as the current was much swifter. They needed to cross by ferry. He got back in the driving seat and edged his wagon back to the trail toward the camp the other wagons were making. He needed to speak to Captain Jones to see what the plan was for the crossing tomorrow.

CHAPTER 41

*H*e settled the girls before going to find Captain Jones. As he approached the man, he got a bad feeling. It wasn't just the expression on his face but on those of the men surrounding him.

"Are we crossing tomorrow?"

"That depends," a man he didn't know replied. "How good a swimmer are you?"

"Swimmer? We are taking the ferry. Aren't we?"

"The ferry broke loose of its moorings the night of the big wind. It was only retrieved a couple of days ago and the repairs are still ongoing. They said it would take at least two weeks, maybe three before we can cross."

"But we can't wait that long. The snows, the mountains." Rick knew he was stating the obvious but he couldn't help it.

"We can't cross the river without it. Have you seen that current?" Mr. Bradley said, the fear in his eyes mirroring that on several other faces.

"We have an alternative but it is not a route I would recommend. We could continue traveling on this side of the river."

"Sounds good to me," Mr. Bradley commented.

"The route is almost grassless, in fact it reminds me of a desert. The oxen and cattle would really suffer, lose a lot of weight and will thus be rendered less able for the terrain up ahead. The lack of water bothers me. But there is another reason. It's right through the middle of a number of Indian camps."

"But the Indians have been friendly."

"They have but it may not stay that way. The young braves are getting annoyed at the number of white people taking over their land, as they see it. The chiefs are finding it harder to keep them in line. I would rather not test their patience."

"So the river is the best option? Aside from the current, are there any other hazards we should be aware of?" David asked.

"There are many hidden holes in the river, which can cause the wagon to tip and roll. We will need to guide the wagons across first before the cattle. Some men will have to stand by to fish possessions out of the river if a wagon over turns or items fall out. Obviously, the oxen are most important so don't try to save a favored possession in place of an animal. If we don't have animals to pull the wagons, we will continue the journey on foot. Not an attractive alternative, specially for the women and children among us." Captain Jones let his words sink in. After a minute or so of silence, he continued, "So we got a choice folks. We cross the river ourselves or we wait for the ferry to be ready." Jones's tone suggested there wasn't much of a choice in his eyes.

"If it gets fixed. There's nobody saying they are going to be able to fix it for definite," David Clarke spoke up, "so my vote is we go via the river. We've crossed dangerous ones before. I'd rather take a chance on the river then take a risk in snow covered passes."

"It's easy for you to say, you ain't got no young'uns."

"True, but I plan on having some. Just as soon as my beautiful new wife and I reach Oregon."

CHAPTER 42

*R*ick admired David Clarke for making a decision but was it the best one? Should he wait for the ferry to be fixed or brave the water? What if Clarke was right and the ferry wasn't fixable. Then they would still have to cross the river but would also face the risk of snow covered mountains.

"I reckon we should take some time to think it over. What will you do, Captain Jones?"

"If the group splits, I will go with the majority vote. I owe it to you all to get you to Oregon as safely as possible. My vote would be to cross the river now. Waiting for the ferry, whether or not it is fixable, increases the risk too much for me. But it's not my choice. I can't tell which way will be safer, so I will stick to my promise to get as many of you to Oregon safely as I can." Captain Jones surveyed the group. "If we choose to cross the river, I suggest we move on until we come to the Three Island Crossing. It's a route taken by many a wagon train before us."

The men nodded then broke away to chat amongst themselves or go consult their wives.

"That's fair enough for me." Rick turned to walk back to his wagon but found David Clarke falling in step with him. "You really think the ferry isn't fixable?"

"I don't know for a fact," David said. "But what I do know is that there are lots of wagon trains in a hurry to cross those mountains before the snows come. The longer it takes to fix that ferry, the longer the queue. I know the river will be difficult but I think it's doable. I would prefer to test it myself but Eva, my wife, won't hear of it."

Rick had only spoken to Eva a couple of times but having got to know Johanna so well, he guessed a stubborn streak ran in the Thompson women.

"What are you going to do?"

"I don't know. I don't have a wife to worry about but I have two nieces. They lost their ma and brothers just after we joined up with your train. Not sure if they are ready for a big adventure." They had arrived at Rick's wagon.

"Want some coffee? I think Johanna left some cake too. She likes to spoil the girls."

At David's cocked eyebrow, Rick allowed a smile.

"I would love some. Johanna told me you lent her a book. You wouldn't happen to have any others, would you? I have a couple we could trade, if you like. I don't get to read much but I like to get a few pages in when I can. Although these nights, I'm usually so tired I fall asleep standing up."

"Yeah I have three. Sit down and I will go fetch them. I want to check on the girls anyway."

Rick left David by the fire as he went to check on Sarah and Carrie. Both of them were fast asleep as was Johanna who seemed to have fallen asleep reading to them. Should he wake her and bring her outside? The man sitting at the fire was her brother-in-law. She might be embarrassed. But if she woke and came out while they were talking that would look worse. It would seem as if he was hiding her presence. His dilemma was answered when Johanna opened her eyes. She sat up glancing her head off the storage box he had resting at the side of the wagon.

"Are you all right?"

"Yes, but I shouldn't be here."

"You must have fallen asleep reading to the girls.

David is waiting for me outside. He wanted to borrow a book."

"David is waiting for me?" She was still half asleep.

"No, he wants a book. Do you want to wait while I get rid of him?"

"No. David will understand I was minding the girls."

He didn't believe her but he didn't argue and went to get the books. Taking them outside he handed them to David. "Good job we came back. Johanna had fallen asleep reading to the girls. Have you read any of these?"

"Evening, Johanna. I took your advice and came to see if Hughes had a book I could borrow. Did you sleep well?"

Johanna gave David a friendly push like you would to a big brother. They were obviously good friends, something that caused Rick to feel jealous. What was he doing being jealous of her brother-in-law?

CHAPTER 43

"What were the men meeting about?" Johanna asked while pouring herself a cup of coffee.

"The mountains." David replied at the same time as Rick said, "The river."

Johanna looked from one to another, amusement fighting with impatience on her face. "It's the river, isn't it? Something wrong with the crossing?"

The men exchanged a look.

"You might as well just tell me or I will go ask Becky to ask Captain Jones." Johanna's tone warned them not to try her patience.

"The ferry is broken. It will take at least three weeks to fix it, that is if it can be fixed," Rick answered.

"So I guess we are crossing in the wagons then?"

Johanna said quietly, her face paler than a few minute ago.

Rick longed to be able to reassure her but what could he say? There was a reason the French-Canadian trappers called the Snake River "La maudite riviere enragee" – the accursed mad river. "Captain Jones knows what he is doing. We will be careful."

"Jones will talk to the group tomorrow then it will be up for a vote," David explained before finishing his coffee. "I best get back to my wife. Want me to walk you back to your wagon, Johanna?"

Rick saw Johanna hesitate. Briefly his heart raced faster. Would she tell Clarke to leave them alone? But then she drank back her coffee and said brightly, too brightly, "Yes, please do. Goodnight, Mr. Hughes."

"Goodnight, Johanna, thank you again for your help."

But she was gone. Only then did he realize David had not taken the books with him. Maybe he had read them all ready. Or had the books simply been a ruse to suss him out. Was he worried about his intentions toward Johanna?

* * *

THE VOTE WAS CAST and everyone opted to cross the river now rather than wait. Far too many of them had heard about the fate of the Donner Party and with the cold chill of the winds from the mountain, they figured there wasn't time to waste.

"It's not so much the current, but the bottom of the river that causes the problems," Rick explained to Johanna when he asked her to mind the girls during the crossing. "Jones said there could be holes, each six or more feet in width, so some of the oxen may be swimming while their counterpart is walking."

"You will be careful, won't you?" Johanna said, trying to keep her voice steady. She didn't want him to know how frightened she was, not for herself but for him. He touched her briefly on the hand.

"I will be fine. You concentrate on yourself and the girls. I think Becky is better prepared to swim. Can you not borrow some of her clothes?"

"I think Ma would prefer me drown than to see another one of her girls wearing men's clothes." Johanna's dark humor lightened the tension a little as they both laughed.

"I think you might be right on that point," David added as he and Eva joined them. Eva's knuckles were showing, her hand was so tightly clinging to David.

"Captain Jones has done this before, hasn't he?" Johanna asked in the hope of reassuring her sister.

"Yes, he has. He has a plan to help avoid most of the

pitfalls. He wants horsemen at each side of the wagon. In addition, every wagon has to have four, preferably six yoke of oxen," David explained. "As some have lost their spare oxen on the mountain, we must share. It means the fitter oxen will do two journeys but there is nothing we can do about that."

"Ma and Becky are already lightening our wagon. Becky said Jones told her it would be better to ditch the stuff we can afford to lose now to avoid running the risk of losing necessities such as our food sources. Poor Ma is torn, she knows she will have to leave some of her furniture behind, but it all has precious memories associated with it."

"My wagon's fairly light, Sadie didn't have much to pack. I might be able to take a couple of things across for her."

Johanna could have hugged Rick for this generous offer.

"Let me go ask her. Thank you."

"My pleasure. Why don't I go with you?"

Johanna saw Eva exchange a smile with David and knew she would be in for some good-natured teasing later, but she didn't care. All that mattered was everyone got to the other side of the river safely.

CHAPTER 44

The current was very strong. The first few wagons made their way across to the first and second island without incident. Johanna drove their wagon with her pa and David riding alongside her. The wagon wobbled dramatically as one of the oxen fell into the holes Rick had mentioned, but knowing what could happen stopped Johanna from panicking. She held the reins tightly and waited until they passed the danger. In time, all the wagons crossed without any toppling over. Johanna exhaled softly, thanking God and everyone else Captain Jones was such a good leader.

Now they just had to wait for the cattle to cross. The animals were proving mulish. They obviously hadn't heard of the dangers in snow covered passes. There was no incentive for them to enter the water. The men herding them shouted louder and louder but without success. The storm that had been brewing all day started in earnest. Sheets of rain poured down making everyone miserable as well as scared.

"They need to get those animals across before we have to deal with lightning and worse," Pa muttered. Just then Captain Jones called for more men to join the others. Johanna held her breath again as David and Rick both volunteered. They crossed the river back to where the cattle were situated. Again and again, they drove the animals to the edge of the river, only for the herd to split and stampede in different directions. Finally, one of the men's patience must have given out or else he was worried about the fact it was nearly dark, but as the cattle moved toward the water, he jumped on the back of the lead ox and drove him into the water. The plan worked, with the cattle following their natural leader. Johanna and the other people waiting on shore cheered in relief as the cattle all crossed over. The last of the men were crossing when lightning suddenly lit up the sky. The thunder that followed was deafening. Johanna looked toward the water to see Rick's horse rear up, obviously petrified. Rick did his best to hang on but another streak of lightning flashed across the sky and the horse bucked again sending Rick into the water. She saw him splashing and then it went dark again as the clouds rolled over.

"David, Rick is in the water. Do something."

David held her back. "We can't, Johanna. Not in the dark, it's too dangerous."

She struggled in his arms but he didn't let her go.

Another flash of lightning lit up the sky. "Johanna, look. He's on the sandbar in the middle of the river. He must have swum to it."

Johanna looked, her heart beating so fast it was making her dizzy. Rick was lying on the sandbar mostly out of the water but he didn't seem to be moving. Was he dead? He couldn't be. Not after reaching relative safety.

"We have to get him out of the water."

Captain Jones came forward. "Have you spotted him?"

"Yes, he's on the sandbar over there. Look. You have to get him out."

"We can't risk it, Miss Thompson. The water is raging now and with the storm it would be too dangerous for anyone to try and swim out there.

"But you can't just leave him."

The look in Captain Jones' eye told her that's exactly what they intended to do. Johanna begged and pleaded but nothing worked. Her ma came forward and half dragged half carried her back to their wagon. "The girls need you. Pull yourself together, girl. This is not what he would want."

"But, Ma, he could be dead. And he doesn't even know."

"Know what? You love him? It's written all over your face, love. He knows."

Johanna didn't believe her ma but she was right about the girls. Carrie was hysterical but she was more worried about Sarah who didn't seem to be upset. She was standing like a statue staring at the water but there were no tears. "Sarah, come with me. We need to find you and Carrie dry clothes and some food. I suspect you are starving."

Sarah didn't seem to hear. She stood staring into the water.

"Come on, love, it won't do Rick any good if you come down with a chill. Please, Carrie needs you."

That seemed to reach something inside Sarah who turned to Carrie, took her by the hand and pulled in the direction of the wagons. But still, she didn't speak. She didn't try and comfort her sister either. It was like she was a stranger.

The night was the longest Johanna had ever experienced. The lightning stopped, thankfully, but she almost missed it. She couldn't see Rick anymore. It was far too dark. Feeling completely helpless she stayed with the girls, Carrie eventually falling asleep on her knee. Sarah just lay there, saying nothing.

"Sarah, honey, please talk to me. You are scaring me now."

"It's my fault he's dead. I told him I wanted him dead." Sarah turned her face away.

Shocked, Johanna didn't know what to say. A few minutes of silence passed only interrupted by Carrie's soft snores.

"Sarah, Rick is not dead. We have to hope he is still alive until we find out different."

"He's dead, everyone dies. That's just the way it is. I wish I were dead."

"No, Sarah, don't say things like that. Imagine what it would be like if you weren't here. Carrie would be distraught and so would I. It would break Rick's heart."

"He doesn't care."

Johanna put Carrie down on the bedroll carefully so she didn't wake her. She inched closer to Sarah.

"He does care. He loves you and Carrie. He is just not very good at showing you how he feels."

"You think so."

"I know so. And I also know he knows you didn't want him to be dead. You were just angry."

"But why does everyone nice die? Ma was kind and

she's gone. Benjy wasn't bad for a big brother. George was only a baby. Pa didn't die and he's really mean."

Johanna gathered the young girl to her, cuddling her tightly. "We can't explain why some die and some live but together we can pray for your Uncle Rick. We can will our thoughts to him. Tell him we are thinking of him and we will see him tomorrow. Shall we do that?"

Sarah nodded and together they said a prayer.

"Now close your eyes and pretend you are talking to Rick. Tell him everything you want to tell him. Maybe he'll hear you in his mind."

Johanna watched as Sarah screwed up her eyes in concentration, her lips moving as if she were talking. After a long time, she fell asleep. Johanna waited, prayed and waited some more. It seemed like daylight would never come.

CHAPTER 45

*S*he must have nodded off at some point as Eva came to wake her.

"David, Captain Jones, and a couple of the other men are trying to rescue Rick now. Do you want to stay here or come to the bank? Becky will stay with the girls if you want to come with me?"

Johanna knew Eva was worried about David going back in the water. Although it was daylight and the storm had gone, the current was still fast. It was a risk.

"Thank you, Eva."

Turning to Becky, she whispered to let the girls sleep as long as she could. It was better they didn't know about the rescue attempt until it was over.

She walked slowly down to the shore, her hand clutching Eva's. She saw the men further out. They had just reached the sandbar. It was obvious from the way they were holding Rick, he wasn't conscious. Was he dead? He couldn't be. She put her head up and made herself watch the rescue. David was swimming on one side of Rick with Captain Jones on the other. Rick was on his back and the men were keeping his head out of the water. Turning quickly, she ran back to the wagon to grab a blanket. She was back before they got up the bank.

Running into the edge of the water, she held out the blanket. "Is he alive? Please tell me he is."

"He is but he's close to death. Get some whiskey. Give me that rug." Captain Jones' gruff tone betrayed his lack of hope.

Johanna's ma came running with the whiskey. She forced Johanna to give the men room to work on Rick. Captain Jones and Pa rubbed it into his body. David trickled it into Rick's mouth but it simply ran out the sides.

"Rick Hughes, wake up now. You are holding us all up," Johanna said fiercely.

As if he had heard her, she saw him swallow. David gave him another small mouthful of the whiskey and he opened his eyes.

"Jo?"

She wrenched free of her ma and sank to her knees

beside him. "I'm here, darling. I'm here. She kissed him all over his face before kissing him on the lips.

"That'll sure warm him up," someone commented.

"Do you think if I went for a swim she'd do that for me?" another man called out.

Johanna knew she was making a scene but she didn't care. All that mattered was Rick was alive.

"Come on, young lady, that's enough of that. Go make your man some hot soup to keep the chills away."

Although Ma's tone was gruff, Johanna knew she was more relieved than upset.

"I will be back, Rick. I have to tell the girls."

"Soon." He closed his eyes again but this time he was sleeping. Johanna walked back with her ma leaving the men to carry Rick. It wouldn't be seemly for her to change his clothes or wrap him up in bed. She wasn't his wife. Yet!

Rick slept for hours as his body recovered from the bashing it had received. Ma and Johanna applied salves to the lacerations on his face and upper torso. Mrs. Freeman, Ma, and Mrs. Newland worked on his legs, insisting it was not appropriate for an unmarried woman to help.

Captain Jones suggested they set up camp six miles north at the edge of the foothills. They had to set off again the next morning to make up for the time lost when everyone had been ill. Hughes would continue to travel in the back of his wagon until he regained consciousness and recovered. Johanna volunteered to drive the wagon and nobody argued with her.

* * *

LATER THAT EVENING, the lecture she'd been expecting from her father started. Ma insisted she come to eat something leaving Rick in Eva and Mrs. Newlands capable hands.

Johanna sat down beside Becky who gave her hand a squeeze. David sent her a compassionate look while Mrs. Long asked her how the patient was.

"He's just the same. He hasn't woken up yet."

"Such a brave nice young man. I will pray for him to recover. And for you, too, Johanna. I didn't realize you two were courting."

Before Johanna could reply, her father answered.

"Neither did I. She's too young to be courting." Turning to look at her, he continued. "You are the talk of the wagon train, Johanna Thompson. Kissing a man in public like that. I didn't know where to look."

"Leave her alone, Paddy. You would have done the same."

"I'd never kiss a man, Della Thompson."

"You know what I mean. If it were me lying there half dead, I would hope you would be grateful to see me alive."

"It would depend on the mood you were in."

Everyone laughed including Ma. Johanna smiled her thanks at her mother. She was still a little in shock. She hadn't thought of anything other than the fact that she hadn't lost Rick. Not that he was hers to lose. It wasn't as if they had an official agreement or even an understanding. Nothing mattered in those few minutes. She loved him and it seemed as if he loved her back. Her name had been the first word he said.

"So how long has all this been going on?" Pa asked, his tone still slightly quarrelsome. "I don't recall anyone asking my permission to go courting."

"We haven't been courting," Johanna protested.

"I know you think I am ancient, lass, but you don't go kissing a man who you have never been courting. At least in my day you didn't."

"We have been spending time together looking after his nieces. But there were complications." Johanna's face burned at having to discuss something so private in front of an audience. Even if these people had become as close as family.

"What sort of complications. He doesn't have a wife, does he?"

"No, Pa, of course not."

"So what is the problem then?"

Johanna stood up. "That is between myself and Mr. Hughes. It is nobody else's business." Although she spoke calmly, Johanna was shaking. She hoped her legs would carry her to her tent. She didn't want to face the embarrassment of falling over.

"Just a minute, young lady…"

"Paddy, leave her be. Can't you see, she's reacting to the shock." Her ma stood and put her arm around her. "Come along, love, I think you need some medicinal whiskey."

"I could do with some whiskey." Her pa's pleading tone made people laugh once more, thus diverting the attention away from Johanna.

CHAPTER 46

*R*ick didn't wake up. Everyone had become more concerned as the time passed on. Johanna could tell her ma was worried even if she pretended not to be. When they stopped for nooning, Johanna sat by Rick's side talking to him but there was no reaction.

"Why won't he wake up, Jo?"

"I don't know, Carrie. He probably just needs a rest."

"I am going to read to him. He kept telling me to practice. I am doing good now."

"I am doing well now, you mean," Johanna corrected her automatically.

"That's what I said." Carrie gave Jo a funny look before turning her attention back to Rick.

David came to help her get ready to move out so she left Rick with his nieces. He would wake up soon, he had too. Almanzo escorted the wagon walking beside it the whole way. He didn't say much but he kept looking into the back as if expecting Rick to look out. Johanna's grip tightened on the reins. She couldn't afford to scare the children so wasn't about to give in to tears. She had to be strong for them and for Rick.

* * *

THE NOT SO GENTLE rocking of the wagon was making his head hurt like the blazes. Why was his bed moving? Where was he? Rick opened his eyes to see both his nieces staring at him. Carrie was still holding the book she had been struggling to read to him.

"About time you woke up. You've been real lazy."

"Carrie, you can't talk to Uncle Rick like that," Sarah reprimanded the younger girl. "He's not lazy, he's been sick."

"He'd tell me off if I stayed in bed all day." The defiance in Carries tone made him smile but it didn't last long due to the painful laceration on his face. He remembered crossing the river and then the lightning. He'd come to as the water went over his head, the current fighting to keep him under. He'd fought for breath before striking out for the nearest piece of land he could see. It had taken every piece of energy he possessed to reach the sandbank and then the world had gone black. He wondered if Spirit had made it back. He hoped so, that horse had been with him a long time.

He opened his eyes again. "Sarah, can you ask them to stop. I...sick." He couldn't form the words properly but saw by the widening of Sarah's eyes she understood.

"Jo, stop the wagon. Uncle Rick is going to be sick everywhere."

The wagon stopped with a jolt. It didn't help his stomach. He tried to push himself up but, thankfully, she was there to help just in time. He leaned out over the side of the wagon as what seemed a river of water exited his stomach. Weak, he slid back against something hard. She leaned over him to dry the side of his mouth.

"Sorry...not pleasant," he muttered.

"You're alive and awake. Don't be sorry. Be thankful." Her eyes glinted with tears but her smile took up nearly her full face. He wanted to kiss her but couldn't. He squeezed her hand instead.

"Thank you. Kiss at river." He smiled as she turned bright red. "Drown again for kiss like that."

She swiped him with her apron. "Don't you dare. I have had enough shocks to last me a lifetime."

"With me?" He knew it wasn't the most romantic proposal, but it was all he could manage for now. His eyes closed but not before he saw the happiness on her face.

CHAPTER 47

*I*t took a few days, but finally Rick recovered sufficiently to drive his own wagon. He tried to get Johanna alone but it seemed their kiss had made her father more protective. She was rarely out of his sight. Rick wanted to propose to her in a more romantic fashion but given the lack of privacy he lost patience. That evening, he walked into the Thompson camp leaving his nieces behind.

"Evening, Hughes, is there a problem?" Mr. Thompson looked at him curiously.

"There is no problem at all, Mr. Thompson other than me being rather slow to make a declaration of my feelings. I love your daughter and nothing would give me greater honor than if she became my wife."

"Well, if that just takes the biscuit. I don't even know

you, lad, and here you are asking for my daughter's hand."

"He's not marrying you, Paddy."

"I know that, Della, but I don't know anything about his prospects. Are you intending on staying in Oregon, young man?"

"Yes, sir but not as a farmer. I wish to set up a school where both myself and my wife will work."

At that Johanna threw her arms around his neck and kissed him.

"Johanna Thompson, can you leave your intended alone for five minutes. We have business to discuss. Mr. Hughes, Rick? You do know she is only turned seventeen?"

"Yes, sir. I am prepared to wait."

"No, Pa, please," Johanna begged her father.

Her enthusiasm to marry him made Rick's heart swell with love for her.

"Ma was younger when you two got married."

"We knew each other a long time, Johanna. It was different. I think it best you two have a long engagement. If you should still want to get married, I won't pose an objection."

"But, Pa..."

Disappointed, Rick had no option but to accept her father's decision. It wasn't as if they could elope. "No, Jo, your Pa is right. You are young and it has all been rather sudden. We will wait until Oregon." Rick offered his hand to Johanna's father. "Thank you, sir. I hope to get to know you and your wife better over the next few weeks."

"Well said. Now where is that whiskey? Della, do you have some left over?"

"Paddy Thompson, my supply is purely for medicinal purposes."

"It is medicinal. I have just had a marriage proposal. Another one. None of the guidebooks mentioned this hazard on the overland trip."

Everyone smiled at the joke. Rick wrapped his arm around Jo's waist as she laid her head against his shoulder.

"Mr. Thompson, will you allow us to go for a walk? I would like to tell my nieces and a certain young man our news."

"What young man?"

"I am hoping Almanzo will agree to become part of our family." At a slight nudge from Jo, Rick quickly added. "That is if he fails to find his own parents."

Rather than look pleased, Rick was a bit taken aback by the look on Mr. Thompson's face. He hadn't imagined it either as Jo said, "Pa, what's wrong?"

"I don't like surprises. Are you trying to tell me that

not only are you starting married life with two little girls but you are adding a boy as well? Just how many children will you be supporting on a teacher's salary?"

Rick looked at Jo who was blushing prettily. Squeezing her hand tightly, he replied, "Well, I guess as many as my beautiful wife to be will give me."

The consternation on Mr. Thompson's face made everyone laugh once more.

Rick knew he better let Mr. Thompson save face. "Mr. Thompson, if your daughter and I are as happy as your wife and you, I will consider myself very fortunate."

"Spoken like a true diplomat. Maybe it's politics you are destined for not teaching, lad." Mr. Thompson turned to his wife and said, "Have you found that whiskey yet?"

Rick took the opportunity to steal Johanna away. He walked them toward his wagon but dipped in behind another one to steal a kiss. Then he went down on one knee.

"Miss Thompson, will you please do me the honor of becoming my wife?"

"Say yes, Jo, please say yes."

Johanna giggled as Rick groaned. Sarah, Carrie and Almanzo stood by, watching them closely.

"We are never going to get any privacy tonight," he whispered.

"You didn't say yes, Jo. You got to do that before you kiss him again," Sarah prompted.

Johanna looked up into Rick's eyes. "Yes, I do." Then she reached up on tippy toes and touched her lips to his.

"Yuck. I'm not ever letting anyone do that to me. Prince or no prince."

Carrie's remark echoed loudly across the camp.

"Come on you two, you should have been in bed hours ago," Johanna chided the girls gently.

"Are you going to turn into a mean stepmother like the one in my story?"

"You never know, Sarah, I just might." Johanna made a face that had the girls shrieking with laughter as they ran ahead to the wagon.

"I wonder if I will ever get some time alone with you."

"Well, you're the one who said we would take on this ready-made family," she reminded him, smiling up into his eyes.

"Do you mind?"

"Not at all, I already love those girls like my own. I love you too."

"I am glad to hear that. If it weren't for you, I would have lost those girls through my own stupidity. I can't believe I ever thought I could give them up to some orphanage."

"I never believed you actually meant to do that. Nobody who loved *Oliver Twist* could do that to a child."

She linked his arm as they headed back to the wagon to their new family. He hoped it wouldn't be too long before they reached Oregon and he could truly claim her as his wife.

* * *

CAPTAIN JONES WATCHED the excitement from a distance. He was pleased for Johanna and Rick. Despite her relative youth, Johanna had shown her maturity over and over. He thought they were a good match and would have a long and happy marriage. He turned his attention back to the girl sitting by the fire, a slight distance between her and her pa. Although she resembled Johanna, she was the clear beauty of the twins. But it wasn't just her looks that attracted him. He had never come across a girl who got under his skin the way Miss Rebecca Thompson did. She was witty, intelligent, kind, willful, brave, impulsive and a whole load of other things he couldn't put a name to. He found himself thinking about her all the time. He checked on her more often than any other traveler in the group. If he was honest, he also came down harder on her than anyone else. He told her off for driving too fast, too slow, for going hunting and for a hundred other things. It amused him she wore pants and a shirt. She wasn't the conventional woman he had imagined he would settled down with. But then, conventional wasn't a word that would ever be used to describe him. He sat chewing on the stick at the corner of his mouth. He couldn't approach her pa and ask for her hand. Especially not after what Mitchell had said. He cursed silently. He'd thought Mitchell had been hanged for his part in the murders at White Point. A group of white men dressed as Indians had attacked a wagon train. Unknown to them a couple of the boys had survived and identified Mitchell and his friends. Last he heard, the judge ordered him to swing. But why had he been set free? And what was he doing at Fort Hall?

* * *

THANK you so much for reading the second book of the Trails of Heart series. I hope you will enjoy the continuing stories of the Thompson girls and the people who come in and out of their lives. The next story is about the third sister, Johanna.

Becky Thompson doesn't take no for an answer.

She knows what she wants and his name is Scott Jones.

Scott Jones's future was stolen along with his heart.

He cannot love Becky, but can he keep her safe?

After months of illness, deprivation and betrayal, with the end in sight have their problems only started? Oregon Destiny

* * *

HISTORICAL NOTE

In researching this book, I came across diaries of Emigrants having issues with their tires. I thought tires were part of the automobile industry and so didn't expect them to be around in 1852.

I was extremely lucky to have a friend who knew someone whose family business was once involved in making wagons. She checked with him and his response was as follows:

"The way wheels were constructed started with the central hub with the stokes and outside wheel parts all mortise and tenoned together from the outside in. The only way to hold it all together was a band to tie it all. So the band became known as a tire."

ACKNOWLEDGMENTS

This book wouldn't have been possible without the help of so many people. Thanks to Erin Dameron-Hill for my fantastic covers. Erin is a gifted artist who makes my characters come to life.

I have an amazing editors, Julia and MacKenzie, and also use a wonderful proofreader. But sometimes errors slip through. I am very grateful to the ladies from my readers group who volunteered to proofread my book. Special thanks go to Marlene, Cindy, Meisje , Judith, Janet, Tamara, Cindi, Nethanja and Denise who all spotted errors (mine) that had slipped through.

Please join my Facebook group for readers of Historical fiction. Come join us for games, prizes, exclusive content, and first looks at my latest releases. Rachel's readers group

Last, but by no means least, huge thanks and love to my husband and my three children.

Oregon Discovery (book 4)

Oregon Disaster (book 5)

12 Days of Christmas - co -authored series.

The Maid - book 8

Clover Springs Mail Order Brides

Katie (Book 1)

Mary (Book 2)

Sorcha (Book 3)

Emer (Book 4)

Laura (Book 5)

Ellen (Book 6)

Thanksgiving in Clover Springs (book 7)

Christmas in Clover Springs (book8)

Erin (Book 9)

Eleanor (book 10)

Cathy (book 11)

Mrs. Grey

Clover Springs East

New York Bound (book 1)

New York Storm (book 2)

New York Hope (book 3)

Made in the USA
Monee, IL
18 April 2022

94927184R00156